THE Hacked MANTICORE
AND OTHER CYBERPUNK STORIES

Nicholas Licalsi

STEP INTO THE ROAD

First published by Step Into The Road Publishing 2023

First edition

This novel is entirely a work of fiction. The names, characters and incidents portrayed in it are the work of the author's imagination. Any resemblance to actual persons, living or dead, events or localities is entirely coincidental.

From this point on take everything with a grain of sale. I made most of it up!

For Samfro, my best friend, thanks for 'hancing my eyes to see the world of cyber punk. Our friendship means the world to me.

Thank You Patrons!

Your generous support and encouragement got me into Galleria Valley and back out with all my limbs attached. I bring these stories back to you in gratitude.

Katelyn Combs, Bonnie, BW, Melinda Callender,
Roy & Beth Shockey, Callen McMillian, Sam Meeks, John Middleton.

Contents

In Over Your Head

T he notification of a new message blocked Bett's sightline of the room. It was addressed to the conglomerate executive he was impersonating but the preview of the first line had his name on it. No one was supposed to know he was here. Opening it could be a trap, but leaving it untouched was an affront to his professional capabilities. He began setting up encryption to protect himself.

Pink and teal sine waves streamed across the dark blue terminal walls of the office. During working hours stock prices and the latest news would replace the screen saver. It was an inoffensive animation and Bett felt it didn't do the company justice. If it was up to him the walls would stream Death Reports so the executive that occupied the office during business hours could be reminded of who he'd killed lately.

A flatworm cable ran from the itchy microfuser embedded around Bett's eye to the desk in front of him. The microfuser had yet to heal. The encryption setup took his mind off of the irritation. It'd be another two hours before he could retake the Clarvo pain relievers. If he retook the Clarvo. The less of it the better.

The less he took the less money execs like... he looked at the desk's name plate... Shawn McNeal would get in monthly bonuses. Shawn...

what a neat name. Just like the neat family pictured on McNeal's desk. McNeal was clean-shaven with neatly combed black hair, his wife was at his side with straight black hair and makeup around her eyes instead of a microfuser. Two girls stood in front of them wearing unwrinkled conglomerate school uniforms. It reminded Bett of high school. He hated it.

Bett was higher than he'd ever been in the Valley. Napalm's bright green car hovered behind him. He could hear the engine through the gap between the window and the wall. The office sat higher than his grandfather's apartment, higher than Bett's 'glom high school. It was certainly higher than the bar they'd discussed this job in.

The fresh air of the night carried wisps of cloud in through the window's gap. An open window hundreds of stories above the streets of Galleria Valley seemed dangerous to Bett. But the War of Acquisition a few decades ago led to strange office design decisions. Like the fact the desk was in a cubby instead of the center of the room.

The office was freezing cold. Not just because the window was open or because the place was unoccupied. Bett had heard rumors that offices were kept chilly because the execs needed to wear full 9-piece suits, three of those pieces being body armor, which kept bullets out and heat in.

Bett on the other hand wore a high-collared neon green raincoat with little insulation and a bulletproof vest that Phlox had gifted him a few jobs back. So far he'd kept the holes in both of them to a minimum.

It was eerily quiet this high in the Valley. No street merchants were shouting about their wares, no gunshots echoing like thunder, no taxi engines zooming past kicking bitter-smelling smog in your face. Bett's chest wasn't restricted by anxiety, despite being on a job. For the first time in a long time, he could breathe easily.

The computer chimed notifying him that the Delauren process had completed and the files he came for were ready. He began transmitting the data out of the security of the office. He put some finishing touches on his encryption and opened the strange message.

Robert, Thanks for the sour gum - QB

Attached to the short message was a cyberton of data. Scanning it for threats he found none. There was too much to read so he sent in summarization bots to comb through it. He'd get the gist of the data in only a few seconds.

Phlox dragged a couch across the office. It wrinkled the rug and let out a deep scraping groan and the feet gouged into the floor. Her broad bionically 'hanced shoulders were locked in place making them appear wider than usual. Napalm leaned on a wall, not seeing any point in helping Phlox. Bett knew the driver's unenhanced torso wouldn't contribute much. Instead, Napalm contributed some moans about her fortifying the office at all.

"If we get pinned down you'll be glad this is here," Phlox said.

"It's a couch," Napalm replied, "it's going to stop a bullet as well as a fly stops a bus."

"It's a 'glom couch." Phlox patted the cushions.

"And?"

"And the cushions are filled with bulletproof stuffing. Desk has some too."

"You done yet, kid?" Napalm asked Bett. The driver didn't help lift a glass coffee table Phlox was now moving but he did reorient himself in the room so the couch sat between him and the door. The door was locked. The trio hoped it would stay that way. But their boss Mack had only promised ten minutes of concealment.

"Just got some files about some Clarvo research," Bett replied. He wasn't sure the summary bots were getting everything right. Some of this data was making radical claims. He looked into the authenticity manually.

"Are you clocked or something?" Napalm didn't wait for the answer to take a sour tone. "We're looking for data about next month's merger. It's going to be bloody and Mack wants an edge."

"That's sealed up like a suit. It's transmitting to Mack now. This Clarvo stuff is..." the authenticity came back legit. He didn't know how it'd wound up addressed to him. Let alone sent to McNeal's desk. Based on the brief of McNeal he wasn't even a part of the medical branch of the Mandlestadt conglomerate. McNeal shouldn't have even gotten it, Bett certainly shouldn't be reading it.

Bett checked the notification again.

Robert, Thanks for the sour gum - QB

Sour gum was a kid's treat. Bett hadn't had it since he dropped out of 'glom school.

"Bett. You good?" Phlox asked. She dropped the glass coffee table on the wall of furniture with a thud. It didn't shatter.

"I knew he'd blow it," Napalm said. "You and Mack put him in over his head."

"He knows what he's doing," Phlox said. "You're not going to blow it, right?"

***

"You're not going to blow it, right?" Phlox asked. She stood between Bett and Napalm, arms stretched wide. Her 'hanced hand was massive, like her shoulders and hips. Her thumb to pinky was the width of Bett's thin frame. Her metal fingers pressed into his chest. "You're not gonna blow up his car."

The private booth at the Ending Theme was becoming conspicuous. Eyes stared and security seemed to apparate from the crowd. The dance music thudded through Bett's body, his back was against a wall with shaggy fur hanging on it. It didn't provide him much comfort.

"Should put a crater in your head here and now," Napalm said.

Bett stared into the dark barrel of the electric blue gun. He was in over his head. His threat slipped out before he could catch it. The burn of the microfuser on his face was making Bett irritable. The computer was under his skin, so he wanted to get under others.

"He's not gonna do anything to your car," Phlox reassured Napalm. "You're not doing anything to his car," she instructed Bett. She lifted her eyebrows encouraging him to take the life preserver she was offering.

"I'm not gonna do anything to your car..." Bett considered adding something to the end of the sentence. Phlox's gaze kept him quiet.

"Let's take a seat 'Palm," she suggested. She grabbed the tall collar of Bett's rain jacket and guided him back to the couch like a dog then sat down next to him.

Bett heard the hydraulics of her bionic chest expand as she stretched her metal arms across the back of the couch to act relaxed.

Napalm holstered his gun at his waist and sat opposite Phlox. The man's hair was dyed orange and cut high and tight with long curls at the top making it look like a cloud sat on his brow. He wore bright red driving gloves that matched his synth-leather jacket. His left eye was surrounded by the metal plates of a microfuser. If he had other 'hances Bett couldn't spot them. They were likely cerebral. As an elevator Napalm would need to think fast to drive fast.

Bett lost sight of the club's security. Scuffles were always good for business. Gave the joint real street credit. But things could go from entertaining to problematic in seconds. Security kept it from getting there. Bett wasn't sure they'd intervene fast enough to save his head.

"You mentioned Mack gave you a terminal with data for the job," Phlox said.

Napalm slung a translucent tablet across the table. Phlox booted it up. The bust of an executive, clean-shaven and neatly combed black hair hovered above it as text scrolled vertically next to the holographic face.

Bett's cheek burnt. He didn't feel like reading the exec's profile. He looked at the terminal's clock, ten minutes until he could dose up again. What was ten minutes? He reached into his jacket to pull out the Clarvo.

Napalm's hand sprung to his waist. "Whatchu doin' kid?" The words came out measured like a dog's growl.

"Relax," Bett revealed the inside of his coat with his other hand to show the auto-IV coming out of his pocket. "It's for the microfuser."

"You're still on that sewage," Napalm scoffed. "Stopped using mine two weeks after the install."

"The doc installed mine today."

"Today?!" Napalm wasn't impressed. He sounded scared. "Mack said yous were crazy. We don't know if he's even stable."

"He's stable." Phlox swiped to the next screen on the tablet. Stock prices on 3D graphs hovered in front of her. The data was more than Bett wanted to parse right now.

"I'm stable," Bett echoed. He rolled up his sleeve to take the meds.

Despite getting the install from a deep doc, instead of a high one, it'd gone well. His mother had a high doc do hers. Under conglomerate reimbursement at that. Hadn't helped.

Phlox put up the cash for the install. She claimed it'd pay for itself with the extra jobs they'd be able to pick up using it. It was the same logic his mom's project manager used. Unlike his mom, Bett held out and didn't jump at Phlox's first pitch.

However, he eventually folded. It was expensive to climb out of the Valley. Phlox took him to the sketchy doc deep in the Valley. Phlox vouched for him; said he was ex-glom. Did her the shoulder and back 'hances after the guy who did her arms got gutter service.

"He hasn't gotten the hang of it. What if he overclocks?" Napalm whined, "The microfuser could get out from under him."

Bett's hand shook as he set the Auto-IV on his inner elbow.

"He's fine," Phlox assured him. "The encryption needs a Delauren process ran on it," Phlox told Bett. "You know how to do that?"

Bett took a deep breath and pressed the start button on the Auto-IV, hoping it wouldn't be the last time. "It's been a while since I ran a Delauren."

RGB lights flashed under the auto-IV running image processing to find his veins. Pneumatic hisses lowered a needle to his skin. The needle, not as sharp as it should have been, went in with a noticeable prick. Bett tried not to gasp.

"We've got a couple starter keys here with the tablet."

Bett failed to stifle the gasp. He felt the cool medicine stream through his veins.

Phlox looked over to him. "You know what to do with them?"

*****

"You've got a couple starter keys here on the assignment," his mother put her finger on the homework problem Bett was working on. "Do you know what to do with them?"

"Of course, I know what to do with them," Bett replied.

His mom's face looked back at him, she smiled knowing the truth. The smile was kind but the face was unfamiliar. Like when his science teacher Mrs. Galia got a haircut last month. Bett knew it was the same person, but his mind took a moment to realize it.

His mother's left eye was ornamented with metal plates around it. They tapered to points as they ran around her skull behind her ear. Her hair was shaved for the procedure and now short hairs grew from her skin. The metal plates, he knew they were small computers, protruded out of her skin like hovercar roofs lifted above the trunk and hood. Except unlike the cars the microfusers were surrounded by red skin. Not red like blood but red like his acne.

Small lights flashed across the microfusers indicating that some process was running. It was likely an automatic process but he didn't know for sure. His mom always focused on people when she talked to them. She refused to multi-process conversations, an inefficiency her manager often chastised her for.

"Why'd you have to get that AI installed?" Bett asked.

"It's not an AI. It is for work."

"Grandpa never had to get one."

"Grandpa was higher up than me."

"Why didn't you inherit his position?" His grandpa had died two and a half years ago. The only things they'd inherited were his high Valley apartment and access to ParaMed insurance plans, both of which were more than his mom's salary could support despite working for one of the biggest conglomerates in the Valley, Mandlesadt. "Bellina says that her father inherited his executive position from his father and someday she'll get to inherit it from him."

"Your grandfather wasn't an executive," his mother said slowly, almost regrettably. She put her hand to her face, pressed the microfusers, winced, and put her hand in her pocket then looked back down at his homework between them. "The keys, let me show you what to do with them."

"He fought in the war. Didn't everyone who survived get to be an exec?"

His mother groaned. Not in anger or frustration. It was the same groan she let out when Grandpa told the stories. "The keys. You plug them into the Delauren function like this," she started putting together a program on his tablet. Explaining each line she put into place.

The tablet was new. She bought it for him so he could take an advanced programming class. The same advanced programming class he was putting off homework for now. "Can't I do this later?"

"No, we should do it now. You've got it in front of you now, easier than trying to dig it up again later." She spun the computer around to him. "Does this all make sense?" She pressed her hand against her face again but not hard enough to wince. She looked at the time on the tablet, then said, "Give me a minute."

"Grandpa always said he should have gotten an executive office. Said we should be higher up in the Valley. But Huntson stabbed him in the back for the position." Bett remembered seeing the scars on his grandfather's wrinkled back every morning when the man made coffee in his underwear.

His mother carried her medicine back to the table and cleaned her inner elbow with a disposable swab. "Did you look over that function I made for you?"

"No," Bett admitted. "But it's okay I'll have an AI on my face like you do if I ever need to do this."

"The microfuser can't write the program for you, it's not an AI." She placed the auto-IV onto her clean inner elbow. "Besides, an AI would be too dangerous to put in your mind." She pressed the button and the machine flashed and hissed. "This is just an assistive program that helps speed the processing time—"

Her arm shook, pushing the new tablet off of the table. The auto-IV stayed in place on her inner elbow but all her limbs shook uncontrollably.

Bett looked at her, the metal plates were no longer the strangest thing about her face. Her eyes were rolled back into her head. The long hair on the right side of her head flung wildly over her shoulders. He rushed to her side of the table, grabbed her arm, and pressed some buttons to release the auto-IV. It wouldn't come off. Her whole body was shaking now. She slipped off the chair.

Bett tried to catch her. She wasn't very big. He wasn't any bigger. There was little that could be done except ease her fall to the ground.

Her head bumped up and down on the rug. It shook like a sonicball, he tried to hold it but it wouldn't stay still. He wedged his legs under her head and shouted at the tablet to call the ParaMed emergency number.

The Auto-IV made some more pneumatic sounds, then fell off the ground with a thud.

The paramedics would be here soon, conglomerate medics showed up fast, unlike Public Health Service. But the emergency line rang over and over. Bett wondered why it wasn't an instant connection. His mother's breaths were shallow. He wondered if he needed to do chest compressions or something like they did in the movies. The medics would tell him on the phone.

"ParaMed ParaMed, we'll help you out, unless you're dead," An automated female voice sang out the company's jingle. "How may I direct your call?" she asked.

"It's an emergency, my mom, she," his voice was frantic, "I don't know. Fell over. I need help."

"There is no policy associated with this account," the automated voice was calm and had an even rhythm.

"It's under Spencer. I'm Robert Spencer. My mom, she's Mia Spencer. We've got a Mandlesadt plan." They'd inherited it from their grandfather, at least the right to purchase a plan above their means.

"I'm sorry the policy for Mia and Robert Spencer was discontinued three months ago. I can connect–"

"No! She wouldn't cancel it. We need medics right now. She needs medical help."

"I can connect you to the Public Health Service," the voice repeated calmly.

"No, I don't want Public Service. I want help right now. There's a policy. We have a policy."

"ParaMed can not send private health care medics to an uninsured household. I'm connecting you to the Public Health Service for assistance."

"I don't want Public Health!" Bett shouted at the tablet. The cursed thing had been nothing but trouble this evening.

The line rang once then a cheap automated voice notified him it'd be ten minutes before he connected. His mother's breath had stopped. He tried the things he'd seen in movies, he pressed on her chest, he blew into her mouth, he considered ripping the foreign computers off her face, but knew it wouldn't help.

When a tele-medic picked up the line, Bett sobbed the story of what had happened into the microphone of the three-month-old tablet, already out of date compared to his classmate's tech.

"I'll send a body crew," the tele-medic said, "Sorry kid, we can't fix overclocks."

***

"We can't fix overclocks," Napalm said. "If he goes bad on the job he'll blow this whole thing. It's not a subtle job but I want to get out with my head on my body."

"He's not going to overclock on the job," Phlox said. "You're not overclocked right?"

"I'm not overclocked," Bett repeated. The Auto-IV dinged in completion and his cheek felt warm instead of hot. Bett rotated his inner arm and caught the medication with his other hand.

"He's a daydreamer," Phlox said. "He gets like that sometimes. Busy thinking about what the world should be like instead of how it is. Right?"

"Sure," Bett said. He could now focus on the tablet in Phlox's hands. She'd seen what she needed to and passed it to him. He looked over the keys to put together the beginnings of a Delauren program to get past the exec encryption.

Computer windows appeared in his field of vision. He looked in Napalm's direction but wasn't focused on the driver. Previous programs he'd uploaded to the microfuser were pulled from his memory. No, not his memory, the memory of the microfuser. He was not the computer. That way lay ruin.

"Careful with that thing kid," Napalm's words sounded slow to Bett's ears. The increased processing speed the microfuser gave him had caused his sense of the real world to slow down so subtitles appeared over Napalm. "Mack put me on this job to make sure you two didn't blow it."

"I knew Mack added you to keep an eye on us. They don't trust me," Phlox complained.

"Should Mack trust you?" Napalm raised one of his eyebrows. The microfuser around his eye didn't move and the skin tugged at the edges.

Phlox gave him a grin. "Bett's not going to overclock. He's a pro. Trained in a 'glom school."

"Still... it was dumb of yous to install it day of."

Bett switched his gaze between the Delauren code and the subtitles of the conversation. Neither was particularly interesting to him.

"Mack wanted a muscle and a hacker with a microfuser. Now we've got both."

"We've got a liability. Most overclocks happen first week of an install or under high-pressure situations. We're putting him in both. Have you even let him get the wheels under him?"

"He's doing that now," Phlox gestured to Bett.

Bett's view of the world was out of focus, glazed over like a donut. The keys did not fit together. Training his program to run around it was difficult. "My mother wasn't using her microfuser when she overclocked." He wanted to give the last word an inflection, but they all came out too quickly.

"Hotshot thinks he can palav while he works. Ripe for an over-clock." Napalm said. "You don't know what your mother was doing in her head. No one knows what overclocks are doing when they seize up."

Bett knew his mother. Knew her well enough that she wasn't going to use her tech while talking to him. She wouldn't even let Grandpa take business calls during dinner. She once threw his terminal across the room when he picked a call up.

"She was dosing on Clarvo."

"Clarvo is a pain reliever, it's harmless," Napalm said. "Took three extra doses a day when I had my fuser installed."

"You're still hung up on that?" Phlox sounded disappointed. "'Hances wouldn't be possible without Clarvo. They made sure it was safe."

"Sure sure, Death Reports say different," Bett's words came out quick and emotionless.

"Death Reports don't say nothing but names."

"And cause of death," Bett added. "Combined with install records-"

"You're not supposed to be running analysis on Death Reports," Phlox said. "You're supposed to be doing the damn Delauren so we can get a last meal before the job."

Bett ran some final unit tests on the Delauren function he'd built. They came back green. "Delauren is done," his voice slowed down to its regular cadence. "Ran the Death Report analysis a few weeks ago. Saw a post on Dark Unity Network that connected some dots between death watch names, their install date, and location of body pickup. It seemed there was no correlation between act-"

"Dark Unity says anything to rile people up," Napalm said. "It's how they get views and money. They just report claims without support."

"They had some data to support it," Bett said.

"Get your head out of the clouds and come live in the real world," Phlox said. "We're getting Stinky's tacos before this job. If I die tonight I won't have to deal with the gas in the morning."

***

"I'll deal with getting fuel in the morning," Napalm said. They were in his hovercar slowly climbing in altitude through the city. Despite being outside the tower it still felt like riding in an elevator. Bett snickered finally connecting the dots on why people at the bottom of the Valley called drivers elevators.

Bett sat in the backseat and it was littered with bed sheets, under-wear, and some hair gel. Napalm allegedly owned the car. But only the richest in the Valley could afford that. Everyone else had to settle for renting public cars. But if Napalm owned it, it'd explain why he worked for Mack. Dependable wheels were hard to find. Even if the car flew and the only wheel on it was for steering.

The elevator was wired in. The flatworm cable shone silver and neon reflecting the city's billboards that flashed between advertise-ments. It ran from Napalm's cheek to the dashboard and connect-ed him to the electronics of the car. He maneuvered through traffic climbing higher in the city with every turn.

The car still smelled like tacos. Napalm had given them a thorough lecture about not spilling anything onto the seats. Bett was careful, didn't want to piss off someone he might be in the thick of it with. Clarvo had reduced his pain and increased his patience. But the car was far from pristine. Music played on the radio, a quick-paced tune about sleeping over at someone's house. It was old and unfamiliar to Bett.

"The lift dampeners of the car, you could really blow those?" Phlox asked Bett through a private message. She was sitting inches in front of him in the passenger seat of the car.

"I'm not going to do anything to Napalm's car," he replied, trying to reassure her of the emptiness of the threat he'd made earlier in the night. He didn't even remember what it was about. He was just irritable from the microfusers.

"Good. You better not. But could you do it to someone else's car?"

"Sure it's just a quick hack job. Most modded vehicles like this one already have cracked governor chips to install upgrades and security bypasses. Usually, modders don't reinstall conglomerate security so it's an easy misallocation job you can bury in the code. Whose car do you have in mind?"

"Someone big. I'll tell ya later."

Bett only knew one person Phlox considered big, Mack. Not as big as some of the execs but big enough to take down Mr. Louise the former kingpin at the bottom of the Valley.

Mack was the only person Phlox seemed to think about on a regular basis. Whether they were old lovers or just bitter rivals, Bett didn't care to know. He wanted to stay on Phlox's good side. And he certainly wanted to stay on Mack's good side. The day he had to choose would likely be the death of him, regardless of the side he picked.

He wondered how they'd write that up in the Death Reports. Probably just another body found in the gutters. He wouldn't be a John Doe though. Not with the microfuser installed. As long as his head was still on when the body crew found him. They could pull his ID off the microfuser and inform the next of kin. If a next of kin existed. Bett didn't have anyone, yet.

He wanted someone. Wanted a whole damn family. Like he was supposed to have with his mom. It's what his grandfather fought for in the Acquisition War. Bett didn't want to live like a rat at the bottom of the Valley. He wanted to be in the towers. One day, he'd earn enough from a job that he could afford to finish up his school work and apply to a 'glom gig. Family connections wouldn't get him far. But as long as he kept his record clean on jobs like this he'd be fine.

"Bett, you there," the message from Phlox popped up over his eye through the microfuser.

"Bad time to go catatonic," Napalm said. The flatworm cable slithered out of his microfuser socket and receded into the dash of the car. The roof of the car retracted and the starry sky was revealed above him.

"I'm here. I'm fine." Bett said.

"We're above the clouds," Phlox said. "You can see the stars every night this high."

Napalm plugged an overloader into the steel siding of the office window.

A breeze whipped up and Napalm's jacket billowed in the wind. It was a strong enough gust that if Napalm was any lighter he'd get carried away. It would probably carry Bett away. He didn't think he'd mind that.

The window opened. No shattering, no noise. Just the silent compliance of a hacked machine.

"Let's go." Napalm gave Bett a firm look. "You know what you're doing right?"

***

"He knows what he's doing, right?" Phlox repeated.

"This Clarvo data is scary," Bett said. The words were quick as his microfuser mind combed through digital reams of data. "They've got clinical trials saying that it causes seizures in over thirty percent of people that take it. It's been this way since before the Acquisition War. They made a change in '57 to save money on manufacturing cost—"

"Focus on the data we came for," Napalm slammed his gloved fist on the desk. The quake knocked over the family picture McNeal kept there. "Can we leave yet? Mack only gave us ten minutes on this then we're on our own."

Bett pulled his mind away from the data and began setting up transmission protocols for it. "The merger data's sent," he said.

"Good let's go," Napalm said.

"I need to send out this Clarvo stuff too," Bett said.

"We'll get it next time," Phlox said.

"No, we should do this now," Bett said. "We've got it in front of us. It'll be easier than trying to dig it up again later."

A seal broke on the office door. Security bots filed in guns pointed at the group.

"We're going now," Napalm climbed out the window and into his car.

Phlox ducked behind the fort of furniture she'd made while Bett hid behind the desk. His flatworm cable hung over the side.

"We'll get this later," Phlox said.

"There's no guarantee of later," Bett said.

Phlox returned fire. It was deafening. His next 'hance would be electronic eardrums like everyone else in the Valley. Muting a sound like that would be a godsend.

The data was less than a quarter of the way through being transmitted.

"Who are you sending it to?" Phlox asked. Her shots disabled the first wave of security bots. But knowing 'glom security there would be more. And eventually, they'd be human which was Bett's biggest fear.

"Sending it to the Dark Unity Network. This is what they needed."

"You think this data's going to get their attention? They get thousands of deranged manifestos a day."

"You want me to upload it to the independent forums. That gets millions of shit-posts on it every day. It'll get buried."

The trials were privately funded, there was no public record of them. If this went on the net a 'glom scrub bot would take it down nearly immediately. It needed to be in twelve places at once. But Bett didn't have the bandwidth or the time. He barely had the bandwidth to send it to the Dark Unity Network.

Human voices shouted from the doorway. They didn't blow in shooting wild like the security bots. They were more careful than that, they were not as easily repaired.

"I'm leaving," Napalm shouted from the car.

"Wait," Phlox shouted out the window then turned to Bett. "How much time do you need?"

At this rate, he'd need three minutes. He didn't have three seconds. But he could change the target. Send this off to the person this transmitter was tuned for.

"Thirty seconds," Bett said as he redirected the data to be delivered to Mack.

Would the mob boss be interested in it? Probably not. But Bett could get it off this computer.

"We don't have thirty seconds," Napalm shouted.

"Hold down the fort," Phlox said. She handed him her gun. "Then get out. I want that pistol back. And I need you for the dampener job." Phlox set an auto turret on the desk. "Waste of a damn good turret," she complained. "You're in over your head here. Always have been. Try not to overclock yourself in the fight."

"I'm leaving..." Napalm shouted as if it was last call at a bar.

"Jump out the window when you're done and we'll catch you," Phlox said as she crawled to the window, staying lower than the furniture.

Bett wondered if they would. But he didn't care. He needed to get the data out. That was the justice his mother deserved.

The turret began firing upon the security personnel as soon as they entered the room. Napalm's car dropped away from the window. Bett looked at the transmission progress. It felt like thirty seconds had passed but that was merely his microfuser processing time. He had to hold out for a little longer.

Bett shot a few rounds over the desk. His microfuser slowed down time enough to help him aim. His shots got the security guards who filed in the door to turn back.

Phlox had put him in a good position. The room was completely different from how it started. Executive offices were naturally defensible positions after the War of Acquisition a few generations ago. The lack of cover from the door to the desk's cubby helped.

But these were trained guards. Bett didn't have the skills to hold them back. Even with the microfuser he was fighting against people with military-grade 'hances. Trained to use microfusers since they were teens playing sonicball.

The auto-turret flew off the desk with a loud bang. It landed in front of Bett with a beanbag sitting on top of it. Bett ducked for cover hoping they'd use the same kind of rounds on him.

He looked at the transmission. It eeked the last millimeter of progress to 100%. Bett shot blindly over the desk as the flatworm cable slithered out of his face.

His blind shots did little to deter the guards. They responded with hundreds of bullets. The window took a few too many hits and crashed out into a thousand little pieces.

Phlox had told him to leap. If they didn't catch him he'd be a splatter of blood washed into the gutters.

If the guards caught him he'd be just about the same.

He ran out the window. Bullets flew around him. He fell towards the clouds below him. His kevlar vest caught a few shots, his body caught a few more.

***

"You're gonna catch him," Phlox demanded. She was holding her second gun to Napalm's head but he didn't seem to mind.

"I'm Mack's best elevator. You crater me and you won't be able to work in the Valley again."

"There are other employers in the Valley other than Mack."

"You won't be able to work because you'll be dead."

"Catch him. He's gonna be Mack's best hacker soon."

"I'll have to do a lot of calculations. It's not as simple as sweeping under him and–"

The window of the building crashed out. Pebbles of glass rained onto the cloud cover.

"Get him!"

Bett flew out.

Napalm's car lurched into gear. His microfuser flashed lights like a dance club. Phlox knew if he was really Mack's best elevator the calculations wouldn't be difficult.

The car glided over the tops of the clouds then dropped. Phlox's stomach lurched up her throat as the car tried to match the speed Bett fell. Then Bett landed in the back seat.

Well, most of Bett landed in the back seat.

Phlox stared at the horror show in the back of the car. Bett's green rain jacket was covered in blood. Everything was covered in blood. Except Bett's head. His head wasn't covered in anything because it wasn't there anymore.

"That damn sewage-head got blood all over my sheets," Napalm said.

"God damn it!" Phlox pounded her metal fist on the glove box. "That kid was good. Could have been great, could have helped me–" She cut herself off. "He was too good."

"Too good for his own good," Napalm said. "You're helping me wash this out. You're the one who insisted I catch him. What are we doing with the body?"

"Gutter service," Phlox replied.

The Beast's Ledger

J-Red stood in front of the seven-headed beast. Every black scale on the seven long necks stood out with perfect precision, which was an improvement over last month when he first found it. The mouths on the long snouts held rows of sharp white teeth that were stained yellow near the gum. The clarity made it easier to avoid the beast's attacks. He hoped this new resolution would keep him from dying too much this time around.

The bright blue laser shield buzzed in front of him, spider web arms connected the plasma defense to the bracer on his right forearm arm. He held Draco VonDumket's Saber of Light in his left hand. Its plasma blade threw neon green light onto the beast's three remaining legs and cauterized stub of a tail. J-Red had defeated VonDumket months ago, earning the sword. For some reason, it was the only weapon that could tame this dreaded beast.

The beast perched on the old magnetic monorail track that was lowered below the brown tiled floor that J-Red stood on. The shattered glass windows, stained with dirt, made an ineffective roof. Rain came through forming rivers in the grout and pooling in slick where tiles were missing.

I-beam pillars that once held balconies up were bent from the monster's claws, causing the higher levels to slope downward. The beast's lair was once a train station but this world had gone to ruin and places like this ran amuck with nasty creatures.

A month ago, when J-Red first explored this area, the lair looked like a cave. That was before the generation was complete. The pillars were blurry stalactites and the roof was an opaque dirty brown. The train station was a nice improvement and J-Red was glad to see the AI that ran this game trying new things. Even if the logistics of a train station this far away from the nearest town strained the in-game logic.

Blue plasma armor, that matched his shield, covered his chest and legs. It'd taken some hits from the beast and the battery was low. At the edge of his vision, where a microfuser screen would be if he wasn't in the game, a stream of messages came through. Some were encouraging, others were encouraging him to be more optimal in his attacks.

His audience was growing. Battles with the Baltimore Beast, named after some of the words found in the simulated train station, were popular this month. No one was interested when J-Red first explored this area. But enough players had explored this area that the AI-generated resolution, and eventually Ki-El fought it in a highly dramatized manner, as was his style, that the scene became popular through the Valley.

J-Red had done his best to this point to add drama to the battle. He'd chosen the wrong sword for the fight, which is why the beast had 7 heads instead of the original 2. He'd let his battery and his health go low. The audience size was large enough to give him a good number of credits from his supervisor, Watchet.

Which is why he wanted to investigate the smell that'd been lingering around for the past few minutes. Every time he fought near an arched hallway he smelled hot dogs. Those were a delicacy of a food, and J-Red's health was low. Killing the monster would maintain his views, but once he finished most people would drop for the night. Dozens of gamers had already streamed that beast's death. J-Red wanted to do something original, or at least interesting to him.

J-Red cast a doppelgänger spell to distract the monster. A mirrored version of J-Red stood in front of the beast, ineffectively swinging the sword and doing its best to dodge its strikes. The beast caught the clone's coattails but failed to grasp anything of substance. An intelligent foe would notice the illusion immediately. The beast wouldn't notice until its gullet failed to swallow the doppelgänger.

J-Red wandered past plastic signs with illegible advertisements for products he couldn't access in this world and couldn't afford in Galleria Valley. He followed the smell of hot dogs down a stone-arched hallway while the beast crashed against walls trying to catch the decoy.

The hallways of the train station were still underdeveloped. As he walked through the blurry stone arches storefronts began to reveal themselves between gaps in the arch supports. The contents advertised in the window were fuzzy around the edges and the AI that ran the game would only resolve them if he investigated them further. It mostly looked like clothing or electronics, both of which would be withered by time in this post-apocalyptic world.

He found a room filled with tables, they didn't look particularly stable. Sitting on them seemed as effective as trying to sit on the clouds above the Valley. Smells came from different stands that were littered around the wall. Some smells were rotten, others were pungent with earthy spices like the rat vendors at the bottom of the Valley.

The silhouette of a person stood behind a number of them and J-Red approached the one that tickled his olfactory sensors.

Echos still came from the battle that was raging at the other end of the stone arch hallway. The chat in the corner of his vision was livid with comments as the numbers dropped. But he noticed a few true fans encouraging him to crawl behind the counter and push against the game's limits. He smiled as he greeted the person at the counter.

"Want meat-sleeve, do ya?" the NPC said. She'd resolved into a female figure, her clothes and hair were loose and wavy but didn't have the fine detail of individual hairs or woven fabric.

Her dialogue was limited and the language was broken. Her intelligence would increase the more J-Red or other players interacted with her. But for now, she knew enough to give him what he wanted.

"Two please," J-Red planned to store one for later.

She pulled some crusty buns out of a metal box, if it was a steamer it was broken by time long ago. Some murky water held the "meat-sleeves" and J-Red wondered if the apocalypse had made the water that way or if that was authentic to the dish.

The NPC wrapped them in foil and handed them to J-Red. He gave her a few coins and noticed his purse was running low. Art did always seem to imitate life. The coins materialized into her pockets. J-Red began materializing the dog into his mouth.

The taste was remarkable. It was simulated to his senses through his microfuser, and would never sit in his belly but he didn't care. It tasted better than anything he'd had in the Valley, not that he'd had many delicacies there. The tubing that held the surprisingly homogeneous meat was crisp and every bite had a snap to it. J-Red didn't know what was in it but if this was the flavor of real meat from olden times he would happily live through the apocalypse to enjoy it.

The AI had the taste of hotdogs down, there was nothing fuzzy or blurry about this. It was a treat it'd been rewarding J-Red and other players with for years. He couldn't eat well out of the game but in the game, he could live like a king.

The chat at the bottom of his vision cursed and jeered him. Either jealous of his ability to get a good meal or just bored and looking for a fight. Some warned him of the sounds but all he wanted to hear was the snap of his treat.

The black scaly beast blew through the stone arch hallway knocking the carved stone bricks, which had come into focus due to his time in this room, towards the edges of the open court. Three of its heads let out a harmonious roar. It tossed cloudy tables to the side as it limped towards him on its remaining three feet. The NPC woman screamed and hid under her stand.

Two of the heads sprung towards J-Red. He transferred his second foil-wrapped hotdog from the counter to his inventory. His handbag of engulfment would keep anything in it for his next life. It was full of junk and he threw an old sword out to make room for the hotdog.

He plopped the last few inches of his hot dog into his mouth. Two of the Baltimore Beast's heads snapped at him. They'd been synchronized well enough so one went for his torso while the other went for his legs.

A black screen with hovering red letters covered his vision. It read: GAME OVER.

J-Red checked the time and dwindling chat messages, the only remaining ones were teasing him for dying such a mundane death. He was happy with the performance, most players were only able to be killed by a single head. It'd be hard to get his numbers back up this late. He decided to end the session.

***

The face mask pulled away from J-Red's mouth and nose with a wet slurping sound. The olfactory sensors, which had crawled deep inside his nose as he played, made his sinuses feel open and empty. The silver flatworm cable that connected his microfuser, and his mind, to the game slithered back to its home in the rented headset.

J-Red stepped out of the gaming booth and onto the factory floor. A grid of similar black phone booth-sized stations sat under the second-floor mezzanine. Smaller, less sophisticated stations were placed at desks in the back. Nearly all of them were unsurprisingly empty this late into the night.

The mezzanine that surrounded the factory floor had a railing covered in yellow and black spiraling paint mostly chipped to show the rusted silver metal underneath. Watchet, the factory's supervisor, leaned on the railing, gripping it with his sage green 'hanced arm.

His baggy cargo pants and jacket were filled with various electronics and tools needed to maintain the old gaming stations. Above the man's glare, his hair was shaved close to the skin on the left side exposing the grey plats of his microfuser. The rest of his hair was greased to the right. It was a standard #52-b 'glom haircut. It was as uninspiring as it was corporate.

The bangs of J-Red's natural ash-brown hair hung limply over his eyes. It was a shame the mask always deflated his hair like this. He pushed it back trying to interlock it with some of the hair on the back of his head that still had mousse in it. He did not have a standard 'glom cut. Hadn't had one for years, instead he used deep Valley barbers to shave and braid patterns into it. But right now it needed a wash, and he looked forward to taking care of that when he got home.

J-red wiped his face on the bottom of his tank top leaving an oily stain from the gaming mask's interface. He slipped on his sandals and insulated vest which hung outside his booth. His 'hanced arms didn't feel the cold anymore but his natural chest and shoulders still did. The arms were an old relic of when he needed two extra digits to operate the old-style controllers. He kept the six-fingered hands now because he was used to the convenience of extra opposable thumbs.

His ten toes always got cold in the sandals but right now they felt cozy in the overheated factory. Gaming booths running during the day made it sweltering hot and the place had yet to shed the heat. Once he left his feet would be covered in wet runoff from the streets. But it was better than sloshing around in cheap boots.

"You coming down here to pay me?" J-Red asked. The stairs of the factory's second floor had gone out years ago, and he wasn't convinced it was a natural degradation of the old building.

"Pay you what?" Watchet barked. "You bombed peak interest and cost us a few thousand credits worth of views."

"I should get royalties on all the views Baltimore has gotten you by now."

"You'll settle for the two cards I give ya." Watchet leaped over the railing and landed on the factory floor. The landing, combined with the weight of the electronics, pulled down his cargo pants revealing the seam between his 'hanced legs and hairy stomach. He adjusted the pants with a grin. J-Red's head cannon was that the man took the stairs out himself so he had an excuse to use the spring-loaded legs on a regular basis.

"Two cards?" J-Red groaned. "Just give me the one temp card like normally."

"Can't." Watchet recited business as emotionless as a cheap AI. "Execs got logs on your playtime and view counts. You did well enough today that I can't hide it. Besides you've played for the past week; it'd look suspicious if I didn't pay you out. I can't have the audit dogs sniffing around."

The man pulled a handheld terminal with a swipe lane bolted to the side. There were only a few devices like this limping around and it was the reason J-Red played here instead of somewhere more reputable.

Watchet punched in some numbers and scanned J-Red's registration card. The cursed card linked every single debt J-Red owed. Most of the debt was the 'hanced arms but there was some unpaid bar tabs, malcompliance tickets, and outstanding rent charges still linked to it. It would be easier to outrun the Baltimore Beast than it would be to avoid debt in Galleria Valley.

"All said and done you've got your protected ten percent on the card." Watchet turned the terminal to face J-Red.

Some damn union years ago had lobbied for a protected ten percent of income to not be pulled out due to debt. The goal was to keep people from starving and freezing on the streets. In reality, J-Red found it just gave people enough rope to wrap themselves into more debt. And that was likely the reason the conglomerates agreed to it.

He read the total on the terminal's screen. "9.37 in credits?! I did over $100 creds in views today."

"Sure, sure," Watchet agreed. "But I've got maintenance and renting costs and I'm allowed to take that off the top."

"You coulda charged me that all week."

"You insisted I put it off, because of unexpected expenses," Watchet said the last in a mock whine. "Plus I can't have you paying off your debt too quickly, you might start streaming higher in the Valley."

"You're insidious Watchet." J-Red swiped his registration card and the pitiful balance transferred to his all-but-empty account. "What's that leave me on the temp-card?"

Watchet's mouth seemed to grin and frown at the same time, but it may have just been the scars of the embedded microfuser that made his mouth look so twisted. "15.21 after other fees." The man swiped a temporary unregistered card through his machine and offered it to J-Red.

"What other fees?" J-Red asked.

"Cleaning fees," Watchet said with a shrug. Watchet pinched the card between two of his sage green fingers. He scissored them to make the card wobble back and forth. "Take it or leave it?"

"Whores get paid better than this sewage you're giving me!" He snatched the card out of the supervisor's hand pinching it with his two thumbs and lifting his middle two fingers at the crook.

"Do some squats to get that butt of yours looking good and you could be in business." Watchet gave him a wink with his unornamented right eye then yawned. "But until then get out of here. I've got to clean this thing and get to bed before first shift comes in in a few hours." He pocketed the old terminal and pulled out a filthy white rag.

J-Red pocketed his cards and went to face the cold trying not to think about the cleaning process of the mask that was just leeched onto his face or the leeching process that just cleaned credits out of his pocket.

***

The narrow hallway stretched from one end of the tower to the other, the sight line only a bit impaired by the concierge desk. It wasn't a particularly high floor, so the small rooms allowed doors to be cramped next to each other. Thin walls let the sounds of fighting and lovemaking echo through the hall. The smell of cheap earthy spiced food cooked for dinner hours ago still lingered around.

J-Red looked at the screen on the apartment door in front of him. In crisp digital letters, it politely informed him that his balance was outstanding and he'd been evicted for not renewing the daily lease this afternoon.

It was supposed to auto-renew. He didn't need to review his registration card to know why that didn't happen. Additionally, J-Red's credit was corrosive like seawater, so the automated system cleaned his stuff out preferring to leave the room vacant for the tax benefits over giving him the comfort of paying late.

He didn't care about the bed or the shower. A few cheap stim pills could keep him awake through his next round in the game booth. A public shower, only a step above sewage, could get him clean enough. But he wasn't going to take that until he got his stuff back.

He stormed down the hallway to discuss the matter with the concierge bot that ran the floor.

A cheap chain link fence ran from the ceiling to synth-wood desk. The desk had a small trough cut into it for passing cards and impounded items back and forth. A rosy metal concierge bot sat behind the desk, graffitied with rude remarks, obscene pictures, and numbers to call for a good time. The wire fence seemed to be ineffective in deterring this. Especially as it had a few obvious repairs to close up cut sections. Behind the desk were scraps of trash small enough to fit through the gaps in the fence and boxes labeled with room numbers.

It was cheaper to buy a bot to handle these interactions than pay a human employee. The execs that ran the floor's management weren't even willing to shell out for janitorial staff to clean the place up. Repairs to security were somehow an acceptable expense though. If J-Red had a writing utensils on him he'd add a line or two to the bot's stupid bald metal head.

"How may I help you patron?" the robot asked. Its large spherical eyes rolled around inside the eye socket but the servos weren't quite calibrated correctly giving the bot a lazy eye as it looked up at J-Red.

"Room 2304-E. I need the stuff from it."

"Your items are in impound it will be a 10.90 credit convenience fee to retrieve them."

J-Red shook his head unable to believe his luck. 10.90 was more than he had on his registration card. But if he used the temp card to pay it the system would suck the card dry applying the income to his debts. It'd be generous enough to leave 10 percent behind. But by his microfuser's math that was a percent of a credit short.

"I see the box with 2304 printed on it. It's an arm's reach away from you. I'm not paying 10.90 for your automated ass to hand it to me." The damn thing was in sleep mode two minutes ago, it's not like it was inconvenient for a bot to move stuff. That's what they were built to do.

"Your items are in impound. You have 2 days to claim them otherwise they will be sold at auction."

There was only one thing of value in the box and he doubted it would make any money at auction. He pushed his hair out of his eyes, it'd once again come loose from its place, he needed a good haircut. But right now it wasn't in the budget.

He looked at a weak part of the fence that had been repaired a few times. Placing his gunmetal hand on the wire he gripped it with his two thumbs then wrapped his fingers around the links. His hands and arms weren't made for strength, but they were better than a flesh hand.

"ATTENTION:" the bot said in an amplified voice, "destruction of Polystand Apartment property is prohibited. Any damage will be added to your account Jarron Elias Renuth."

J-Red considered pulling on it. Letting the servos and hydraulics rip the whole frame off. The concierge bot wouldn't chase him. The thing couldn't get out of the chair it was bolted to. But the fine could follow him for years through the Valley.

He shook the metal fence hard, the rattling sound echoing down the hallway. The rosy metal concierge bot repeated its warning. J-Red let go in frustration.

"Just one item out of the box, how much does that cost?"

"Fee for impound is 10.90," the bot repeated.

"I'll pay you 5 creds directly, no need for Polystand to know about it."

"Fee for impound is 10.90."

Damn bots couldn't be bribed. Probably paid for themselves in that feature alone. "What if I get a bucket of seawater and splash it through this fence."

"Destruction of Polystand apartment property is—"

"I know, I know. You useless heap of scrap metal just hand me the damn box."

"Fee for impound is 10.90," the bot repeated its cheap automated voice grated against J-Red's nerves.

The bot could go at this for the short bit of night left and well into the morning. J-Red could barely stand two more seconds of it. He needed to come up with 10 cents of credits registered or not if he had any hope of getting things under control.

He pulled his hair back out of his eyes. What he needed before anything else was some food. The simulated hot dog had whetted his appetite for something salty.

***

J-Red fell backward out of the barstool. Flailing his arms back he caught himself and the metal in his arms made a loud clank against the metallic tiled floor. Pressure sensors peaked then flattened out with a pain filter in his microfuser that kept him from screaming. A lesser arm would've broken at the wrist. But his arm hadn't thrown any errors yet.

He touched his right cheek, the guy had been kind enough not to punch his left side and damage the microfuser. The cheek was tender but not bleeding. Would likely leave a bruise. The guy had also been kind enough not to use the full force of his 'hanced arms. Like a silver-tongued executive navigating a board room this man knew how to speak with his fist.

J-Red looked up at Mr. Speaks With Fists who now sat in J-Red's seat. The seat's new occupant didn't spare a glance down. But he was 'hanced head to toe, even his hair was a silver helmet-like mold that merely imitated hair. It was stylish because it was expensive, not because it looked good.

If J-Red retaliated he'd damage his hand by punching Mr. Speaks with Firsts' chiseled titanium cheeks. The indifference towards J-Red was likely performative. With that many 'hances it was unlikely J-Red could attack unnoticed. The guy probably had a dozen cameras in his head running analysis in the back of his mind just to monitor threats.

Worst part was that J-Red hadn't even gotten to finish his drink. Well, what he'd claimed as his drink. An old whiskey someone left behind and the auto-barman hadn't cleaned up yet. But now it was in a puddle on the floor mixing with discarded peanut shells and other liquids spilled earlier in the night.

The view from the floor was like being in a jail cell. Silver metal legs of stools and chairs crossed his vision. The music was a little bit better than what they played in jail and twice as loud. Waitstaff darted between the tables, chairs, and moving patrons. Some even managed to avoid him on the floor without missing a step, as if he was another obstacle to be dodged. Screens hung from every wall playing sonic-ball matches, news reports, or other streamers. Most of it was replays, nothing was live this late in the night.

J-Red preferred this bar because it was always open until the hazy sunrise that filtered over the Valley. The auto-barman was an outdated model that didn't track which drink belonged to which patron. It was a place he could get free drinks and free peanuts and all he had to do was put up with a little disrespect. And that was all he could afford right now.

"You need help up?" A woman asked. She was as thin as a walking staff. Her hair, a #103, was a curtain of loose black curls that hung past her shoulders. It was one of the go-to styles for executive wives, and not cheap because of it.

Her face had makeup on it, instead of a microfuser. There wasn't a 'hance on her body. J-Red was confident with this assessment because her gossamer silk robe clung to her body and hid little.

She offered her soft fleshy hand to help J-Red up. Ivory tattoos were barely noticeable on her porcelain skin. They covered her hand and arm in an intricate sleeve of geometric patterns. Metal arms couldn't be tattooed like that.

There was only one reason someone that unenhanced could wander around a bar like this. J-Red knew he couldn't afford her services for the night, nor could he afford to get wrapped up with whoever brought her here in the first place.

He grabbed her arm for help, connecting his the two thumbs on his right hand around her wrist like a bracelet.

"Thanks!" He smiled at her and used his left hand to pull his ash-brown hair out of his eyes. His hair wouldn't get out of his way.

After a second try, he realized it wasn't the hair's fault. He looked at his hand. "Sewage and seawater!"

Mr. Speaks With Fists turned his head subtly at the curse. J-Red walked towards the door in an attempt to avoid having another conversation with the bully.

"What's wrong?" The unenhanced woman asked.

J-Red held his left arm out in front of her. His six-fingered hand hung limply on the end of it. She grabbed each thumb, then flipped his hand over palm side up. Worried he'd drag her along because of how tight she gripped his thumbs he stopped walking.

"Look I..."

She placed the back of his hand in her palm and grabbed a dirty fork off a table with her tattooed hand. Using J-Red's vest she wiped off the remains of a greasy meal.

"Pinch the top three," she told him.

J-Red gripped the tines with his thumbs pinching as hard as the 'hances allowed. She bent the fork against them leaving one tine up like a pointing finger.

She jammed the fork into his wrist. He winced in response.

It didn't hurt. Merely a phantom reaction from ages ago when he had flesh there. She twisted and turned and J-Red looked around to see who he might be getting in trouble with.

No one seemed particularly interested in them.

Hydraulics hissed in his arm as the woman let go of his hand. It dropped limply on his wrist in a direction it wasn't supposed to.

She shrugged and threw the bent fork on the ground.

"Thanks for trying," J-Red said.

"Come on. I've got better tools in the back." She turned and started walking away from the front door.

"I can't. I appreciate it but—"

"It's free." She nearly sang the words. She looked over her shoulder at him. Her eyes were brown with a gold ring running through the middle of the iris. "You come here because you like free right?"

J-Red couldn't argue with that. If she could fix this it'd be better than having to pay Watchet or worse a deep doc to repair it. He weighed her alluring offer against the threat of getting involved with whoever protected her around her. He followed her.

She led him to a room labeled 'Private' and while he was worried about not being able to afford any services she could provide his concerns were dismissed when he saw the inside of the room.

The woman gestured to a high-backed well padded swivel chair behind a desk covered in glass tablets, various guns, and a few bionic limbs. She pulled a small red toolbox off of a high shelf, it was out of place compared to the kitchenware, woven bags filled with peanuts, and boxes of liquor bottles that filled the racks.

An old synth-leather couch lumpy and stained with age sat across the room. Terminal screens with security camera views of the bar hung over it. Overall the office was hardly bigger than a game booth.

"I'm Sophia," the woman said as she flung bionic arms, hands, and feet towards the couch. She placed her toolbox on the table, then gestured for him to place his arm next to it.

"J-Red," he replied. "How do know how to..." he gestured at his hand.

"I'm a deep doc," she said as she took a screwdriver to his palm and lifted up the gunmetal plates that protected the inner workings. "You couldn't tell?"

Deep docs, in J-Red's experience, usually had 'hances. Hands with fingers on fingers and entire operating tables that they could flatworm into for surgeries. The only similarity she shared with a doc was a room full of scrapped bionics.

"I kinda assumed..." he cut trailed off uninterested in offending Sophia while his hand was in pieces in front of her.

She took a soldering iron out and cranked the temperature dial-up. "You assumed I was a prostitute?"

"Yeah." J-Red winced as she shoved the hot iron deep inside his wrist. Once again, it was a phantom reaction and he felt nothing and she heated some chip deep inside him.

She fed solder into it and white smoke drifted out of his hand. "Sometimes assumptions are correct. Dad was a deep-doc who forbade me from getting a microfuser by the time I could go against his wishes... well I was making plenty of money without it."

She put the soldering iron away and filled a pen with 3D filament. "Need to patch a few more things up with this printer."

"Thanks."

"No problem. I enjoy little jobs like this, never really outgrew the rebellious teenage phase."

"Do you normally snag patrons from the front of the bar and perform services on them back here?"

"I don't think I'd consider you a patron. You didn't buy a single thing tonight and our auto-barman estimates you've eaten at least one of those 12 kilo bags of peanuts on your own to date."

J-Red whistled impressed with himself. "Is there a leaderboard? Because that's one I might actually be on top of."

"Try moving your wrist back and forth slowly," Sofia said.

It was strange to watch the inner pistons of his arm move without a cover on it but everything seemed to be working fine.

"Roll it around."

It felt good. He rolled his other wrist in comparison. It certainly felt better. Sofia went to patch it up.

"Didn't think the barman tracked drink owners. Usually, they get mad at me for snagging orphaned drinks and make me buy my own."

"The boss turned that off for the same reason they leave peanuts out. Claims it's to lure in lost souls who can serve as assets on various gigs." Sophia put the final screws back into place on his hand and gave it a little low five. "I think the boss does it because they always made the most of food they found as a kid and wanted to pay it forward."

"How sweet of them." It didn't pay to have a heart this deep in the Valley. Most who could afford it got theirs replaced. "By gigs, I'm not assuming you're looking for musicians?"

"More like robberies, heists, merger brawls, grave robberies, and light corporate espionage."

"If one was a lost soul who could serve as an asset, could they make a few creds doing it?"

Sophia smiled. "I'm paid well for my assets." She moved her shoulders and hips to make her gossamer robe shimmer. "But you'll have to ask Mack." She gestured at the screen.

Three people all built like barrels were walking towards the back office. If there was a crack in the room J-Red would've crawled through it to get out. He needed ten cents, not a criminal record.

"Oh." J-Red suddenly felt like he was lying prone before a dragon. "Mack, the warlord Mack?"

Sophia laughed and it was bright cutting through the low bass of the music that came muffled through the door. "They'll like that one. Yeah that Mack."

The door slid open with a beep. Unenhanced, as all the stories said, Mack stood framed by the doorway and the two enforcers behind them. They had a #26 haircut dyed a non-standard green. They wore a tight leather jacket with a silver metal zipper running across their body.

Mack looked J-Red up and down, saw the toolbox on the desk and Sophia behind it.

"Out of my chair." Mack flicked a finger ornamented with bright green nail polish.

J-Red scurried out of it and towards the door not turning his back to Mack. He'd been caught in a dozen caves with a dozen monsters while streaming games. But this paled in comparison.

The two enforcers ducked under the doorway to enter the room. A man and a woman both broad in the shoulders and thighs with their enhancements. They had boxy metal hands and one had a microfuser around each eye to manage his 'hances.

"Thanks," J-Red said. "I'll be—"

"He wants a job," Sophia interrupted.

Mack looked at his six-fingered hands then took a seat on the office chair. They kicked their heavy-soled black boots up onto the clear spot of the desk where J-Red's arm was. Sophia climbed up onto Mack's lap making herself comfortable.

"Good, we need a replacement hacker. Take a seat."

J-Red looked at the door, then the couch. It was still covered in bionic limbs. He headed towards the door, "I really don't need one. I was just—"

The woman gently placed her heavy metal on his shoulder. The heavily enhanced man singlehandedly lifted the entire couch up and dumped the parts on the floor.

"Boss says sit," she led him to the couch and sat down with him stretching her enhanced shoulders wide across the back of the couch.

The man sat next to him. The couch squeaked under his added weight but didn't fold.

J-Red didn't need the broad metal shoulders on both sides of his face and the thick metal thighs pressing against his knees to know he was in a pinch.

***

J-Red didn't know much about hacking. He couldn't write a Delauren function. He couldn't convince an AI to self-destruct. If he could he'd have his stuff back and wouldn't need this job. But Mack had found something for him. He wasn't sure if he was grateful for that or not.

His six-fingered hands enabled him to quickly input data through a keyboard. His early days of streaming video games were built on that edge. He had gotten the expensive six-fingered arms for that purpose, hoping to rise up the leaderboards and the Valley. Until everything changed in the industry and tabletop controls went out of fashion.

But the VR experience did teach him to monitor for threats in his surrounding area without any high level 'hances. Which was key because those high-level 'hances would not be approved by conglomerate temp agencies. Mack had contacts at those temp agencies, contacts that could get someone into a data input job at the Baumein conglomerate, but Mack lacked the person with just the right amount of 'hances. Until J-Red walked in.

So now, at 7:30 in the morning, wired on stim-pills, J-Red transposed from a glass tablet projecting a hologram of data into the Baumein system. But it wasn't Baumein stats. It was Mack's data. Data that wasn't supposed to be there, and would throw off any merger plans.

The desk they assigned him was short, less than a meter wide, and made of plastic. The chair was too short for him and too cheap to be adjustable. The only thing that fit him was the six-finger keyboard and even that would start causing his hands to cramp up if he spent too long using it. The cheap setup made the outdated tech at Watchet's look desirable.

The sea of employees to his left and right all wore the same black suit with white dress shirts regardless of their gender. He wore a matching one, although his had more wrinkles.

Each employee had approved 'glom haircuts but nothing more expensive than a #34. And he could only find one of those. J-Red had done his best to pull his unruly hair back into an approved #12 ponytail. But a close inspection would reveal his non-standard braids and undercut.

Mack had assured him that no one would care what he looked like. Sitting at his desk in this sea of sameness he had his doubts.

Most people in the corral were transcribing data from the holographic pop-up of glass tablets. The tablets dropped from a shoot above, nearly indestructible despite being glass, and a timer started on the computer to make sure employees weren't too slow at the input.

There were a dozen reasons this could and should be automated. J-Red wasn't interested in understanding the conglomerate's logic. He was busy transferring both the recently dispensed glass tablet and the glass tablets Mack had given him.

Mack needed the data in before lunch. At J-Red's current rate, it'd be done by his first approved coffee break.

The instructions were simple: type the malicious data in, incinerate the tablets as he went, and pass out 5 credit temp cards if anyone got in his way. Inside the inner pockets of his jacket he had a stack of glass tablets, and opposite them a stack of plastic cards in his left. He wasn't getting paid much for the job, it'd be more profitable to run with the 5 cred temp cards. But that'd upset Mack, and deep Valley stories made it clear that was a bad decision.

Data input was a job J-Red could do, it might even make him enough to pay off the arms in this lifetime. But he didn't have the credit score or the family connections to get in the door. Even data entry was gate-kept by connections.

"Employee 154." A young man in the familiar black and white suit and a microfuser around his eye stood next to J-Red's desk and knocked on it like it was a door. His hair was cut like a #26, tight fades on the side from bottom to top with neatly combed hair parted to the left, but it had grown out a little past standard.

"Yes sir?" J-Red stopped his typing. His metallic fingers trembled picking up neuro noise from the stim-pills he'd taken.

"Our reports show that you're behind on your input rate."

"I've completed each tablet and tossed it into the incinerator before the timer ran out." He'd done his best to burn down the timer to just a few seconds. But he always got the data input in time to avoid unwanted attention.

"Those timers are for your five-fingered friends," the manager lifted his hand and wiggled his flesh fingers. "With your abilities, we expect the data input at least a minute faster."

"Yes sir," J-Red replied quickly. He turned back to his current tablet.

The timer hadn't stopped since the manager walked up.

"Additionally," the manager continued, "there were some concerns about your appearance."

"Yes sir. That will be fixed tomorrow." J-Red kept working on his tablet input. He was under the minute mark but could make it up if this guy would leave him alone.

"I'd like your attention when discussing opportunities for improvement. I like to know that you're taking your position here seriously."

"Will you stop the timer?" J-Red found this guy somehow more frustrating than Watchet.

"Oh yes, of course." The man's tone was polite but brusque.

The timer stopped and J-Red turned to face the man. The lights on the manager's microfuser shimmered. "As I was saying your appearance reflects on the entire Baumein conglomerate. It's important that you match the standard of the rest of the corral."

"Yes sir. I'll do better tomorrow." J-Red repeated.

"Of course you will. But what are you going to do to fix it today?" The manager looked down at J-Red in his too-short seat and desk.

"Would you like me to go get my clothes dry-cleaned right now?" J-Red asked with words as sour as kid's gum.

"No, no, no," the manager said with a laugh. "I would prefer you do it during your next break."

J-Red groaned, then stifled it.

"If you're not interested in matching the standards of the Baumein conglomerate I'm sure your," with a flat hand he gestured from J-Red's head to feet, "rustic appearance would suit Mandlestadt conglomerate's low expectations." The lights on his microfuser flashed.

"I'll take care of it on my next break," J-Red reassured the manager. He didn't have the money for a quick dry clean or a new uniform.

"Best get back to work," the manager gestured at the screen. "Your timer is back on."

J-Red looked and immediately started typing. The timer had slipped a few seconds from where it was paused. He took a time penalty on the tablet, running over and cursing the manager for the distraction.

Three tablets later, each one done with over a minute to spare, a young woman, who seemed barely old enough to graduate from a 'glom academy rapped on his desk.

"Yes, ma'am?" J-Red said without looking up from the data he was copying. It was one of Mack's tablets. The timer had just started for a newly dispensed one but he had hoped he'd built up a buffer of good performance. He didn't know what this manager could add that the previous one hadn't already pointed out.

"Has anyone talked to you about Baumein's attire standards?"

"Yes ma'am they have." J-Red hurried to get the data entered from this tablet.

"I would like to discuss those standards with you right now. With your undivided attention."

"I'm going to take care of it on my next approved break."

The manager leaned over his desk. Her arm got in the way of viewing the tablet. "It's very important that you understand Baumein's attire standards."

J-Red looked at her, her tightly braided hair ran in rows down her scalp and hung off the back. A #19, difficult to do well. Most deep Valley residents would ornament the ends with beads. J-Red doubted that was approved for Baumein's attire standards.

The look on her face was more familiar than the haircut. He'd seen it on Watchet's face dozens of times. His bank account never appreciated it.

J-Red shallowly grinned. "I understand that it's important to match Baumein's high standards." He slipped a temp card out of his jacket's inner pocket and set it on the desk next to her hand. "I hope to rectify the issue soon."

She placed her hand, ornamented with long nails and white tips over the temp card and placed it in her inner jacket pocket. She looked like he'd done something as routine as ordering a drink. "Don't hope. Do. We would hate for this to be a recurring issue." She smiled and winked then walked away.

After the fourth manager of the day came to visit J-Red got into the habit of immediately pulling out cards and placing them on his desk without looking up from his typing.

The stack of cards, which represented more physical money than he'd ever seen in one place, slowly dwindled. But luckily Mack's pile of glass tablets disappeared into the incinerator faster. With the cards, no one reminded him to get his suit dry-cleaned, and he got the job done by lunch.

Walking out with the herd of employees headed to lunch, he still felt a few cards left in his chest pocket. He could buy a hot boxed lunch on the high Valley corporate floors with them. His stomach urged him to. He didn't think Mack would know how many bribes he'd handed out.

Remembering the drink and peanut stats that Sophia recited to him last night he didn't want to test out how much Mack knew and didn't know. Even without a microfuser, he could tell the boss held plenty of knowledge behind their eyes.

***

Mack dealt the remaining stack of temp cards into two piles on the desk of their office while J-Red pulled on the rest of his street clothes, glad to be out of the suit. It'd gotten him some shifty stares walking through the deep Valley to the bar.

He wiggled his toes in his sandals as Mack put the last card on the first stack. It was an uneven number and Mack pushed the shorter stack across to him. It was three cards, not bad. Not quite enough for a hot lunch on the corporate floors but it'd get his stuff out of impound.

Mack swiped another temp card through a hand terminal with an old-style swipe mechanism on it. "Your payment for the job," they handed him the temp card. "I put a few extra creds on it, consider buying a drink on your way out."

He'd rather spend the extra money on a hot shower than a drink. "Thank you, ma'am," J-Red second-guessed himself unsure if he'd said the right thing. "Thank you, sir?" he stumbled over his words still not confident.

"Thanks, boss, is what you're looking for." Mack kicked up their feet on the desk and rested their head back on the chair closing their eyes. "Let me know if you want more work. But for now, get out so I can sleep."

J-Red didn't have to be told twice and found his way out of the den and back to Watchet's shop. He was late for his shift but over thirty credits richer for it. His hair was a mess, the humidity of a cloudy afternoon in the Valley, the grease from the gaming headset, and being pulled back into a ponytail had all done their worst. It flopped in and out of his eyes as he walked.

He decided to take a detour on the way to Watchet's. He wasn't getting a game booth this late in the day, all the streamers that had shown up on time would get those. Might as well take a shower.

He looked down at the rose metal concierge bot with its obscene body art. "Impound for 2304-E," he slipped his registration card and the temp card Mack gave him into the trough under the chain link fence.

The bot came to life and looked at him with its off-centered eyes. It fumbled with the cards as it inserted them into the handheld cash register.

"Your balance has been paid, all things are in order. Would you like to purchase a room for the night?" The bot picked up the impound box and dumped the contents into the gap under the fence.

"Your brain's a calculator, can't you tell from my balance I can barely cover impound fees?" He greedily grabbed the tin can that clanked out of the box. The old T-shirt, hand terminal, and zippered portfolio of tools were unimportant.

"Sir, your balance includes enough money for a full night's stay in our finest room. My upsell circuits require me to offer it to you." The bot showed the handheld cash register to J-Red.

Mack had said there were a few extra creds. Even after 90% had been taken out he still could've gotten a drink and more at the bar. Apparently, crime paid in the Valley.

"I could stay a night or two. But not in your finest room." He had no doubt that even the nicest place here fell short of Baumein standards, and he was never that picky. "A small bed and a shower. Ideally, a room without a cracked mirror this time, unless that costs extra." He twisted the lid of the tin can open.

"Very well sir. Room 2306-E has been updated to accept your biometrics." The balance of the temp card fell to nearly zero. J-Red was glad he still had the 5 cred cards.

He looked forward to the shower and fixing his hair. Then he'd get to Watchet's and explore the hot dog stand more. It wouldn't be a popular stream. But he didn't need to do popular streams with money in his pocket and a place to stay.

He unscrewed the cap of the metal tin he'd rescued from impound. It'd been smuggled in by his barber two months ago. It was non-standard, a relic of times before standard haircuts.

Using it would never be approved on the Baumein attire standards. But it worked on his unruly hair and made it look better than any of the numbered styles in the 'glom's haircut catalog.

J-Red buried his nose halfway into the nearly empty tin. It smelled like citrus covering up musty petroleum notes. Most importantly the smell wasn't simulated by some headset. The gel was in his metal hands ready to tame his hair.

Hive Mind

Thick red and black wires ran in neat parallel lines across the floor of Kiran Galloway's small cell of an apartment in Excella Tower. Empty tin cans once filled with battery acid were stacked in a small half wall around the toilet. A pallet of full cans, stacked as orderly as when they'd been shipped, blocked the front door from opening fully. It was the only place they'd fit at the time.

As neat as everything was organized the apartment was still cluttered and a mess. Kiran mirrored the organized mess of his living quarters. His thick overalls were bleached in spots from acid and had two patches on the legs from where the angle grinder cut through them a few weeks ago. Only three of his dreadlocks had been singed by the bunsen burner. Since then he'd made it a habit to tie his hair back with a thin red wire before starting the day's work.

Two 3D printers squeaked and whistled near the far wall. They printed a fresh batch of parts. They took up most of the small makeshift table, once a pallet used for shipping chemicals, the rest of the table had a pizza box.

The pizza box was unfortunately not nearly as filled as the table, or apartment. Three cold slices covered in artichokes and pepperonis sat in the box. Kiran didn't care. They tasted just as good cold as they did fresh.

He took a bite out of one and leaned against the table. It shifted underneath his modest weight. A few more screws would fix that. Using his microfuser he added it to the ever-growing to-do list that hovered on the left of his periphery vision.

The pizza, just like the battery acid, printer filament, and tools showed up when he needed them. Which used to be strange, three months ago when it started.

Now he came to expect it.

After he finished the pizza for dinner, a new box would come for breakfast. Always pizza, always artichokes and pepperoni. Not his favorite combination, but free food was free food. He couldn't afford to turn his nose up at it.

He couldn't afford much more than sewage and seawater since he lost his job three months ago. The day before the first two packages showed up outside his door.

The original boxes weren't addressed to him. They weren't addressed to anyone. The only marking on the two cardboard boxes was a yellow cartoon bug striped in black ink, and it wore a crown.

He didn't know what kind of bug it was at the time. He knew it wasn't a cockroach, maggot, or fly, those were the kinds of bugs he was most familiar with in the Valley. He looked it up and eventually learned it was a bumblebee.

The packages sat outside his door unclaimed for four days before the landlord started complaining about it. Phrases like "blocked the walkway", "fire hazard", and "lowered the property value" were thrown around.

"I don't care if they belong to the Syndicate's boss or a Baumein board member. You're storing them in your apartment," the liver-spotted landlord shouted when he'd finally caught Kiran keying into his apartment after a failed day of job hunting.

Kiran didn't want to cross board members or mob bosses. But they were a distant threat compared to the landlord who would happily evict him as soon as the week's rent came due.

He dragged them inside and left them still sealed next to the door. Whoever they were for was not going to be able to blame him for snooping in their private shipments.

By the next morning, two more boxes sat in front of the apartment door. Each time Kiran moved a pair inside two more showed up.

Every day.

Two by two.

Industrial cardboard stamped with a crowned bumblebee.

Kiran neatly stacked them in his small apartment. No need to upset the landlord.

The only place to sit in the cell-sized studio was the commode. The only flat surface was the wings of the cracked pedestal sink. Furniture beyond a used mattress wasn't in the budget. So Kiran used the boxes as tables, chairs, a bedside table, and eventually, upon the delivery of two boxes the size of coffins, a bed frame to get his mattress off the ground.

In less than a week his room was finished like a penthouse. Yet the boxes kept coming. Kiran didn't know what to do. He wasn't going to open them and seek the wrath of whoever had input the wrong address when ordering the mysterious boxes. Whoever it was obviously had money, how else could they afford so much stuff? And in Kiran's experience, anyone with money in the Valley was someone he didn't want to upset.

He stood firm in his policy of keeping the boxes sealed.

Until the pizzas arrived.

The delivery bot didn't have much to say on the matter of who the pizzas were for. The boxy black machine stood emotionless. Its roll-up door was lifted exposing the warming compartment. Two steaming boxes of pizza waited for Kiran to remove them. He tried to explain to the bot it had the wrong address. The machine was somehow less understanding than the landlord.

"I didn't order these," Kiran protested. The bots recorded their delivery, he'd be on camera stealing this delivery.

"Dominion pizza, delivered without delay for unit G237," the machine repeated in its cheap sing-song synthetic voice.

Kiran grabbed the pizzas in frustration and slammed the door while the bot rolled off to its next delivery. He placed the pizza on the big cardboard box that was his kitchen table and waited.

Surely whoever was delivering this crap to the wrong address would come knocking when their dinner didn't arrive.

He lay in bed waiting. His stomach growled. The savory cheese and salty pepperonis filled his apartment with an alluring aroma that wasn't the typical backed-up toilet or the musty week-old laundry.

The next morning he opened the box and ate the whole pizza cold. He'd never had artichokes before. He liked them. They had a nice meaty crunch to them.

Without a job, he didn't have money for food. He didn't know when he'd last scrounged a meal together. At least a few days ago. The pizzas that survived the night didn't last more than an hour into the morning.

Tilting open the aluminum door to the apartment's trash shoot he dropped the empty boxes inside to destroy the evidence. With a satisfying clank, the shoot's flap closed.

An hour later another delivery bot arrived. Its warming compartment exposed two new boxes of pizza delivered for unit G237.

This time Kiran took them without question. He ate a fresh slice and left the rest on the cardboard table. Then he cut the tape holding his kitchen chair closed. No one was coming for these boxes.

He might as well know what he was harboring.

Once all the packages were unloaded Kiran wished he hadn't looked. It was more useful as furniture. But by now the boxes were in the trash since there was no space for the empties in his small cell of a room.

Spools of wire, plastic filament, a few kits for printers, and two toolboxes littered Kiran's apartment. It all meant nothing to him. He could sell them individually, might have to so he could make rent, but he wouldn't know what to charge nor did he have the social network to find a buyer.

When the bell of his apartment rang he yelped. Whoever'd ordered this stuff finally discovered their mistake. That was just Kiran's luck.

Kiran used his microfuser to check the peephole camera embedded in his door. No one stood at the door. No packages either, which was an improvement. But this deep in the Valley people were tricky. He kept the chain attached to his door, cracked it open ready to shut it behind him in case he needed to retreat.

Two glass tablets smooth like river stones sat at the foot of his door. They weren't stamped with a bee, weren't stored in industrial boxes, or steaming like a pizza. But there were two of them, so he knew they were related to the recent shipments.

The tablets held a cyberton of data, untraceable and hidden from the highly monitored public networks. He connected to them with his microfuser. Data was transferred wirelessly and a small to-do list appeared on the left side of his field of view.

He was used to seeing transparent windows over his vision, it all but covered his vision when he used to work in data entry. Opening the first task on his to-do list he found a tutorial for connecting to and operating the toolbox. Once it was linked to his microfuser all he had to do was imagine the tool he needed and the drawer that held that tool would slide open.

He worked his way down the to-do list. Most of the early tasks were completing trainings on the tools then it moved on to assembling the printers. There were more tasks than he could do in a day. The overwhelming workload felt familiar.

Kiran had earned a degree for completing the public seminars, free pre-recorded lessons that were cutting edge four generations ago and certified him to do little more than data entry. And he didn't have the connections to maintain a data entry position, hence the recent firing.

These tasks were more organized, and advanced, than anything he'd watched in those old seminars.

With no luck job hunting and nothing else to fill his day, he spent his days knocking off tasks. If he could learn to use the tools he could use the raw materials to make something useful to sell for rent money.

Three months later he still had no idea what he was building. But the landlord hadn't bothered him for rent and he had access to all the artichoke pizza he could stomach. He quit throwing out the packaging material, and when heavy pallets of battery acid were delivered he unloaded them and used the cheap compressed plastic lumber and his new skills to build some halfway decent furniture.

Kiran was running out of tasks on the to-do list though. He'd completed the whole task list of the first tablet a month ago and was cruising through this tablet's list faster since he was now familiar with the tools of his trade, even if the trade itself was a bit obscured.

He knew he was building an array of batteries, the acid he'd mixed and placed in custom-printed cells gave that away a week ago. Although it took a few hours of research to be confident. Whatever guardian angel was sending him pizza and covering his rent wasn't interested in helping him understand the details of his project.

Much like the shipments the purpose of a battery this big was a mystery. The generators from the mines powered every tower in the Valley. An apartment full of batteries would barely nudge the scales.

Self-sufficiency in the Valley hadn't existed since the planet's first colonists centuries ago. And even then it only existed if you conveniently forgot the original settlers' dependence on the numerous conglomerates that funded their exploration. As powerful as the battery was it would only power a few floors of this tower for an afternoon at best.

A battery without a load was like a microfuser without an eye. Both were decorations of questionable aesthetics.

Kiran added a few screws to the table, but it didn't make it any more sturdy. He found a small board from an old pallet and connected it to two of the legs as a cross brace. That helped more than anything.

He crossed it off the to-do list with a thought. Less than a hundred tasks left.

"Connect the MOSFET array to the surge coupler," the next task read.

He'd installed the surge coupler last week, it was a port the size of his fist with nine holes in it. He'd yet to receive a part, or designs for a part, that would fit.

He did a second scan of his loose equipment. Cylindrical stacks of empty filament spools make makeshift workbenches around the edges of the apartment. Three plastic rods with locking sockets at the end lay unused on them. There hadn't been a single task referencing these pieces after he built them, so Kiran set them to the side.

He looked for the data sheet attached to the task to check what he was looking for. No datasheet existed. That in and of itself was strange.

When he needed to learn how to use the circular saw a video was linked to demonstrate. When he needed to print a new part 3D models would appear to help him slice the layers and generate directions for the printer. He never wanted for information.

Except for now. The MOSFET array was a nine-pinned void that he didn't know how to manufacture. Sewage, he didn't even know what it did. He moved on to the next task.

It was dependent on the array being installed.

Along with the next nine tasks.

"Yoooo, Kiran," a voice message from his friend Detroit came from the speaker of his microfuser. "Let's meet at Ending Theme tonight. It's payday!"

"Can't. Busy." Technically the truth, but also he wasn't getting cash from this job so he couldn't afford to go out.

"Too busy to run up Lilly's tab? She got the data log laurel and said the first three rounds were on her."

"Lilly got a laurel?" Kiran scoffed. That was nearly as unbelievable as someone as unemployed as him being as busy as he was.

"We haven't seen you in weeks. Let's party!"

Kiran was at an impasse with the project. Maybe some drinks would give whoever was shipping these packages to him time to get him the MOSFET array.

"I'll be there," Kiran agreed. "With pizza."

He slid the pizza box down the trash shoot. The orders seemed to be scheduled by when he trashed the case. New pizza would be here within the hour.

"Leave the artichokes off this time they taste like sewage," Detroit groaned.

"Pick 'em off and I'll eat 'em," Kiran said as he slipped out of his overalls and tried to find something in his laundry pile that was clean enough to get him into the club.

***

Kiran set the empty shot glass onto the bar top as the music's bass shook his chest. The liquor tasted salty and smokey and added a light burning to his chest. He wasn't buying, so he didn't get to pick, nor did he get to complain.

His pizza box sat on the bar with half of a pizza in it along with a pile of artichokes that his friends had peeled their slices. The group was in a small corded-off section of the bar, nothing as fancy as a private booth, but less public than the dance floor. Ending Theme was packed, unsurprising for a week ending with a payday.

So far the night had been calm. Only one scuffle broke out in a private booth. Some skinny kid got pinned to a wall by a gangster with red hair in the shape of a cloud. The broad-shouldered woman with them calmed everyone down and security disappeared as quickly and subtly as they'd arrived.

The room was just bright enough that you could see what you were doing but Kiran's unenhanced eyes were struggling to keep up with the dance floor's flashing lights. It was difficult for anyone to talk to each other and Kiran had to lean close to anyone or privately message them via his microfuser.

Most of the people here wanted to communicate with their bodies. Including Lilly who was standing close to Kiran shouting up to his ear about wanting to dance.

Lilly barely came up to Kiran's chest even in the heels she wore tonight. She had white hot hair cut short and it seemed to reflect the neon lights of the club.

Kiran noticed that her smokey eyeshadow seemed to reflect the lights in places as if it had glitter in it. An intricate vine-like pattern of fine black lines was drawn around her microfuser and her bare right eye. The decoration made it look like she was wearing an eye mask.

Kiran would be happy to dance with her, he was glad to be out of his cell. It was everything afterward that made him hesitant to agree to Lilly's proposal. Detroit and the others were headed to the dance floor invigorated by the drinks and likely a few other things outside of Kiran's budget.

A drink bot appeared from the crowd around their private section of the bar. A metal platter was welded to its chest with two orange drinks resting on it. Kiran ignored the bot until it passed into the corded-off section of the bar and stood in front of them.

He didn't know what Lilly was up to. He'd told her multiple times he was done hooking up with her. But Lilly had selective hearing, a feature that didn't require electronic eardrums.

"Two hive minds for you Mr. Galloway," the bot said. Its metal was a scuffed ruby with smeared graffiti that someone had tried but failed to fully clean off.

"You shouldn't have Gallows," Lilly said as she picked a glass off the bot's chest.

"I didn't order these," Kiran protested.

"Neither did I," Lilly said with a shrug. She smiled as she sipped the drink. "They're delicious though... is that synthetic honey in it?"

"Off-world organic honey," the bot corrected. "Mixed with mezcal, Italian style aperitif bitters, and lemon juice."

"Off-world honey," Lilly said, clearly impressed. "We should have you cover the next few rounds. What are you doing these days?"

"Who ordered these?" Kiran asked the bot.

"You placed the order. Please take your drink, sir." The unwavering nature of the bot was unfortunately familiar to Kiran.

He scooped the second drink off the platter and the red bot disappeared into the crowd to serve someone else another overpriced round. Kiran looked around the bar, in hopes of finding someone interested in him taking the free drink. The dual deliveries usually helped but in this case, locking him into a conversation with Lilly was not doing him any favors.

"We miss you in the bullpen," Lilly said, "but I'm glad you're doing well at your new job. Let me know if there are any openings."

Kiran doubted there would be. "I miss the group too. New work keeps me busy. My apartment's a mess."

"So's mine," Lilly replied. "But it's better than my hallway. Last week it had so many boxes in it that I had to climb over them like I was a kid at a jungle gym just to get to my apartment door."

Kiran nodded, familiar with Lilly's constant complaining and exaggeration over nothing. It had been a staple of his data entry job. He sipped his drink. She was right, it was good. Sweet and smokey with a sour and bitter note in the end to round it out.

"They all had a little bee stamped on them. You know bees are what make honey. Maybe all those crates were filled with jars of honey," Lilly continued.

"Wait, did the bee have a crown?" Kiran asked.

"Sure there was something on its head. How'd you know?"

"Something similar was happening on my floor," Kiran said with a shrug. "This was happening at the apartment next to yours?"

"No, two doors down and across the hall." She finished the last of her drink. "Come on. Finish yours and let's dance."

Kiran swallowed the last of the drink, it wasn't difficult the drink went down almost like juice, and set it on the bar. Kiran was frustrated. He found himself once again wanting to go home with Lilly. As bad an idea as it was he felt like he needed to meet whoever else was getting these strange shipments.

***

Making it back to Lilly's apartment wasn't a problem. Getting out of Lilly's apartment was the difficult part.

Once the bar tab ran too high most everyone agreed to go back to her place to drink whatever was in stock in her liquor cabinet. She mostly had cheap booze which everyone but Kiran appreciated for its alcohol content, not its flavor.

Much like Lilly's liquor selection, her apartment wasn't great. But it was better than anything Kiran could call his own. The apartment was a pre-furnished one-bedroom place with walls that weren't made of cinderblocks, or at least had been covered so the cinderblocks weren't immediately apparent.

Her kitchen was a table surrounded by cabinets. No appliances, only the rich could afford time to cook or hire a cook. Like most of the people in the Valley, Lilly ate convenience food that she could fit between her shifts or get delivered to her after a long day of work.

Lilly sat close to him on the couch. Two other friends had passed out on the sitting chair and the other end of the couch. A music video played on the screen wall across from them. Something with lots of neon that flashed only slightly less than the lights at the club.

Lilly was uncomfortably close to him. Kiran was pushed to the edge of the couch, the arm of the couch dug into his ribs, the padding hardly did the job it was supposed to.

The only way to get away from Lilly was to get up from the couch. But there wasn't anywhere to go.

Detroit and three others were gambling at the table. They played breaker a fast-paced game of cards that Kiran always lost at. They were no doubt overclocking their microfusers and hyped up on pills. Kiran didn't have any money to lose though and therefore wasn't welcome at the table.

The other rooms of the apartment were already occupied. Two or three people had disappeared into the bedroom an hour ago and based on the sounds coming out of it they wouldn't be leaving anytime soon. Someone threw up and passed out in the bathroom and so it'd been out of commission for the past thirty minutes.

The only escape was the front door.

And that seemed rude.

"Kiiiran," Lilly whined, "why aren't we friends like we used to be? You're always so busy. You never get back to anyone."

"I'm just busy."

"I knooow that. What are you so busy with? You don't have a job."

"I do too," Kiran lied.

"Nuh-uh. Detroit looked you up in all the major departments. You're not listed in any of them. Which means you're doing something elicit? Have you fallen in with the wrong crowd?"

Kiran looked around the busy apartment. He didn't think that would've been much of a fall.

"Are you working with the Syndicate?"

"No!"

"Yeah, didn't seem like your type. But suits higher up in the Valley wouldn't take you." She wrapped both her arms around his and rested her head on his shoulder. "We'll take you though. We all like you. You know that? You don't have to avoid..." Lilly seemed to drift off to sleep. The lights on her microfuser continued to flash so she was thinking about something.

The makeup around her eyes had smeared and the intricate lines she had earlier were now blurred. Her cheeks were flush red from the drinks. For a minute she looked peaceful and Kiran remembered why he'd gotten involved with her years ago.

"I've seen sewage better looking than this hand," Detroit shouted pounding a hand on the flimsy kitchen table.

Lilly startled awake and looked up at Kiran. She leaned in for a kiss. Kiran backed his head away as far as he could.

When Lilly realized his lips weren't where they were supposed to be she opened her eyes and looked at him angry. "What's wrong with you?"

"Nothing I just—"

Kiran didn't know which words to string together to cool Lilly down. She was drunk and high and he didn't want to get involved with her again. Even sober Lilly was like hitching yourself to a speeding hovercar. You never knew where anything was going or if it's ever come down.

"You ignore me for weeks. Then you buy me a drink, come back to my place. Your messages are more encrypted than inter-tower mail."

"I didn't buy that drink!"

"Sewage!"

"Honest to the elders."

"Then who did."

"I wish I knew I—"

The bell of the apartment rang and cut Kiran's explanation short. He was grateful since he didn't know where it was going.

"Go swim in sewage!" One of the card players shouted at the door.

The dismissal didn't stop whoever was at the door from ringing again.

"Whoever it is better have food," Detroit said. "I'm so hungry I'd be willing to eat pizza with those damn leaves on it." He threw his breaker cards down on the table and walked to the door to answer it.

Kiran hoped that it wasn't pizza. The only thing that would do is get him in more trouble with Lilly. She'd think he ordered it on his microfuser to escape her advances. He hoped one of the passed-out partiers ordered something and forgot.

Lilly's microfuser flashed as she checked who was at the door. The color drained from her cheeks. "Don't open that Detroit. Go away," she said.

Kiran was almost grateful for the second statement until he realized it wasn't directed at him.

"Both of you. Get out of here," she said. Her words echoed from the other side of the front door.

Muffled protest came from the hallway.

"I didn't send either of you jack."

"Who is it?" Detroit asked.

"Spindle and Bryce," Lilly groaned.

"Perfect," Detroit responded. "I need someone I can beat at cards." He opened the door before Lilly could protest.

Spindle, a thin guy with 'hanced six-fingered hands for faster data entry, and Bryce, who was also a bean pole minus the 'hances, both flowed in. They passed Detroit with barely a nod and walked into the living room.

"You said we could patch things up," Spindle said.

"That's what you told me too," Bryce added.

"I didn't tell either of you lead heads anything of the sort," Lilly responded.

"You said there was a party, I should come by, we'd have some fun," Bryce said.

"I wasn't drunk enough to be so stupid I'd message you. I told you both we're through," Lilly shouted. "I don't want either of you here." She stood up from the couch and tried, haphazardly, to corral them out.

The only one who moved towards the door was Kiran. He felt bad for the guys, he'd gotten similar messages from Lilly in the past. It'd been heartbreaking when he realized she only meant half of what she said in the messages. Then he noticed the pattern and quit falling for the bait. Surely these guys would learn eventually.

"We could be good Lilith," Spindle continued as Kiran nodded at Detroit and slipped out the door and into the hallway.

"You bring better pizza next time," Detroit called after him, "and some money to lose on breaker."

"We'll see," Kiran said counting doors to figure out which one had been receiving the bumblebee shipments.

He rang the bell on the door, hoping it was the right apartment, and that it wasn't too late at night. The door unlocked immediately as if the resident was waiting for him to arrive.

But the man who answered seemed disappointed to see him. He had long brown hair pulled back into a bun and was wearing a grease-covered jumpsuit, scruffy stubble covered his face. The hand that wasn't holding the door open held a large wrench.

"You a delivery boy?" He asked. The microfuser around his left eye flashed as he looked Kiran up and down.

"No. I uh also have been getting deliveries though."

"You and everyone else on this floor," he said starting to close the door.

"Deliveries with a bug stamped on it."

He looked at him suspiciously. "What kind of bug?"

"A bumblebee. He wears a little crown." For a moment Kiran was sure he'd picked the wrong apartment.

"Yeah, the queen bee!" He said and stepped out of the way of the door to let Kiran in. "I've been waiting for you to show up."

The room was almost identical to Lilly's apartment except instead of being filled with drunks it was filled with empty boxes and electrical equipment.

"You were expecting me?" Kiran asked. "Are you the one sending me the shipments?"

The man laughed. "No. No one knows who's responsible for that. But there's a few of us around the tower that are getting shipments. I'm Amaranth." He threw the large wrench to the couch where it landed with a clank against other tools that were piled there.

He leaned against the table opened a box and pulled out a muffin. "Lemon poppy seed?" Amaranth said holding the treat out to him. "I get two dozen every day."

"I get artichoke pizza," Kiran said taking the baked treat out of the man's hand. "Two of 'em at a time."

"That sounds about right. If it comes in a pair it's from the queen."

"How do you know it's a queen? Could be a king?" Kiran took a bite of the muffin, it was like nothing he'd ever had before. It was moist and airy with tiny pops of crunch from the little black seeds in it. This was nothing like the dry prepackaged muffins he'd pick up from the vendor machine on the way to work.

"Good right?" Amaranth said with a smile. "Bee hives are always run by a female queen. Males are only produced for mating... Actually, it's not important. What do you need?"

Kiran picked at the bottom half of the muffin. It wasn't nearly as good at the top but he still enjoyed the treat. "How do you know so much? Are you a bee tender?"

"Beekeeper. And no, not anymore."

"Wait you're from off planet?"

"It's complicated. What are you here for?"

"I just heard you got packages and I wanted to meet someone else who was getting these shipments. You said there are more of us?"

"Yeah, all around Excella Tower," Amaranth closed the muffin box walked over to a crate, and began pulling junk out. "I met Quai and his brother when I needed a dozen sprockets. They met Vicki with no eyes when they needed some sort of motherboard." With a loud groan, Amaranth heaved out a box the size of a head and dropped it on the ground with a thud that certainly woke the downstairs neighbors.

"It goes back in a chain all the way to Devin Hackborn," he continued. "She's been stuck looking for her antennas going on six months now. So, odds are good, you need... this." He pulled out a black plug with a long cord coming from the end and thin brass prongs coming from the other.

"Is that a MOSFET array?" Kiran asked.

Amaranth shrugged and tossed the thing across the room at Kiran who dropped the mostly empty muffin wrapper to catch the device. He counted the pins, and sure enough there were nine of them.

"This is it," Kiran confirmed.

"Dope. Figure out what you're building yet?" Amaranth waded through the mess he'd just made around the crate and leaned against the arm of his couch. "I've got a generator, Quai and Vicki haven't figured out what either of their machines do yet even though they're done with their to-do lists."

"An array of batteries," Kiran replied. "I'll be done by next payday now that I have this."

"Great," Amaranth said without much enthusiasm.

"You?"

"Same or sooner, unfortunately. Most of the group, except Devin, are done or on the same timeline." He licked his teeth then let out a loud sucking sound.

"You don't sound excited about that," Kiran said trying not to react to his host's unsettling noises.

"I love baked goods but," Amaranth picked at one of his teeth with his pinky nail, "poppy seeds always get stuck." He inspected his finger seeming proud of whatever success he'd accomplished then wiped his hand on his greasy jumpsuit. "Do you know of Noah?"

"Is that an exec?"

"A myth. He built an ark on God's command. God sent him every animal, two by two, to protect them from a flood."

"What's an ark?" Kiran asked confused by the man's tangent.

"A big boat. Impossibly big some might say. Anyway, the flood came. It wiped out all life on Earth except Noah's family and the animals on the boat."

"Why would he kill all those people?"

"They were allegedly irredeemable," Amaranth answered.

"And the animals were irredeemable too?"

"Unavoidable cost of doing business."

"God sounds like a dick," Kiran replied.

"He is," Amaranth agreed. "But do you think Noah was happy when he finished building the ark?"

"Sure. People used to believe in gods regardless of their deity's flaws, gaps in logic in their sacred stories, and they blindly trusted them for their own comfort," Kiran replied. No one believed in gods anymore, humanity had answered all the questions religion was invented to solve. Humanity conquered the universe with that knowledge. And with enough money a Board Member could conquer death itself. "I imagine this Noah guy felt like he'd meet a quarterly data entry objective on or before the deadline."

Amaranth looked at Kiran with eyes that seemed old enough to watch this myth itself, despite the guy being in his late thirties at best.

"The flood killed Noah's friends," Amaranth said. "It drowned his livestock, destroyed his house, washed away the graves of his ancestors."

Kiran shrugged. "It's a made-up story."

Amaranth rolled his eyes and picked at his teeth absentmindedly. "What happens if you meet a quarterly data entry objective before its deadline?" he finally asked.

"An exec will double the scope of your next objective or lay off half the team. Or both." Kiran had seen it done multiple times, and a few months ago he was on the unlucky half of the team.

Amaranth gave Kiran a knowing gaze. "Yet people still finish early."

"Sure. What are you gonna do? Defy an exec? It'd be easier to defy a god. Better to bust your ass and prove you deserve to stay employed."

"And all we can do as members of the queen bee's hive is hope that we're allowed on the boat when the flood comes. You want some muffins?" Amaranth picked up the box and handed it off to Kiran who gladly took them.

"Thanks. I'll bring you a pizza sometime."

"No thanks. I don't do artichokes." Amaranth said with a toothy smile as he led Kiran to the door.

***

On the elevator ride down to his cell apartment Kiran was added to a private group forum that included Amaranth, and the nearly dozen other people who were receiving packages from the queen bee. They called themselves The Hive.

As tired as he was from the long day of work and late night of partying he wanted to knock off a few tasks that hovered in the left-hand edge of his view. Now that he had the MOSFET array he'd be able to finish the battery array in no time.

He summoned the tools he needed from the toolbox using his microfuser to access the correct drawers. He placed them all on the makeshift workbench that was just a few large empty spools of filament knocked on their sides.

He cleared off three plastic rods with locking sockets at the end of them. Their copper core poked out ready to be plugged into some machine Kiran didn't have.

Leaning the long delicate pieces against the wall he reviewed The Hive's forum. People had posted missing parts. All of the threads had been resolved except for Devin Hackborn's. She needed antennas. Three of them.

Kiran looked at the three antenna-shaped rods in his small apartment. He took a picture with the microfuser. Maybe he had the last and missing link in this chain of worker bees.

As he prepared to post it to the final thread on the forum he wondered if he should.

If Amaranth was right and finishing whatever they were building would bring some flood he'd be better off tossing the rods in the recycler.

But could he really stop a flood?

Maybe for once, he could build something that benefitted him, instead of mindlessly processing data for an executive. And hopefully, there'd be enough room on this ark for him. Otherwise, he'd once again be washed out to the bottom of the Valley.

But who else would be caught up in the flood? His friends, Lilly and Detroit. His liver spotted landlord, if he was lucky. But not the executives in their high towers.

Nothing ever touched them. If something did touch them it'd have to be big.

He sent the photo and specs to Hackborn. He hoped the flood was massive. He didn't care if there was room for him on the boat. As long as whatever was coming was big enough to reach the executives and board members in their penthouses. If he was lucky they'd get dragged into apartments as small as his cell.

Making the Most of a Rat

Galleria Valley bustled with activity from the penthouses to the food courts where you could find a deep-fried version of any vermin unfortunate enough to be caught. This evening Mack was lucky enough to be chewing on one of those vermin, it was probably a rat, maybe not. Nonetheless, it was calories not grown in a vat and Mack earned the treat. It wasn't easy for an unlicensed kid to earn credits reliably, but Mack thought they'd finally cracked the code.

Mr. Louise hired Mack to rifle through the apartments of the dead before his Rounders came to clear the body out. Most of the stuff Mack brought back was labeled fancy trinkets and dropped in the recycler. But Mr. Louise found enough to award them a few credits on a temporary card. Those credits bought a fried rat, and would soon buy a shower and noise-proof sleeping pod.

"You're a grave robber," said a boy with a soft chin and a patchy beard of light hair. He might be a few years older than Mack, but they still thought he'd lose if the two fought.

"Everyone I've ever robbed's been alive," they replied nibbling the burnt bits off the skewer. Most people didn't get this bit and Mack had made many meals by hanging out near a vermin stall collecting old skewers to nibble on for dinner. They always made the most of a good rat.

"I saw you," the boy continued, looking down on Mack. "Coming off level 34 D. A scoundrel like you didn't have any business over there."

"Report me to the badges if you care so much," Mack replied poking the tip of the skewer wondering how far they could sink it into the boy.

"It isn't right, stealing from the dead."

"They weren't going to be using it anymore," Mack said pushing their shoulder into the boy's and heading down the street.

After catching his balance the boy started after them. "There are proper channels, the stuff's supposed to go to family and then redistributed."

"Proper channels ain't done nothing for me lately," Mack said depositing credits into a shower stall. The boy wouldn't follow them into there.

The only positive thing about the shower was that it was warm. For about a minute. The grout and tiles were stained so badly that Mack figured the auto cleaner broke a few months back. The soap dispenser was empty and the wet and dry sections didn't seal properly so their only pair of clothes got wet. But it got the grease out of their hair and the layer of grime off their body in a way using a run-off pipe's water couldn't. Mack stepped out of the shower stall to find the boy still waiting there.

"You're low on money, I get it," he continued unabated.

"I got plenty of money," and for the first time, they weren't lying.

"I can help you make some, you don't have to resort to grave robbing."

"They ain't in a grave."

"It's honest work. You're strong, the docks need strong workers."

"Docks?" Mack scoffed. "I ain't got the training for that."

"There are scholarships and apprenticeships. That's a problem that can be solved."

"Get cratered," Mack snarled. They knew enough characters of Common Tongue to get by but not enough to be an apprentice.

"You could make a life for yourself on the docks," he pleaded as the pair arrived at the wall of sleeping pods. "You could rise higher in the Valley."

Mack swiped their temporary card at the terminal. After selecting a noise-proof pod the terminal rudely showed the remaining balance and it was less than half a credit. A platform lowered down to raise them to their home for the night.

"How are you going to sleep soundly after doing what you did today."

Mack shrugged, it'd never been much of a concern to them.

"Find me," he said pushing a scrap of paper into their hand, "There's no future in a life of crime."

"Don't know if there's much of a future in anything I do," Mack said making a fist over the piece of paper. The platform lurched off the ground gears squeaking under the strain of lifting them. Mack dropped the trash once the platform made it up a few levels of pods. They hoped it'd hit the boy in the forehead as he looked up but the cold night wind had other plans. He watched it land next to his feet.

Mack crawled into the pod and locked it behind them. The room was unsettlingly quiet. They rested the disposable skewer near their hand in case of the unlikely scenario someone bothered them in the night. The metal touching metal echoed in the small cylinder. The room wasn't all that different from some of the cracks Mack slept in growing up. The mattress had just as many questionable stains as one you'd find in an alley, and the room had the distinct smell of sex. Above all the silence made it hard to sleep. They longed to hear some street vendor call out keeping them from letting their guard down.

Mack thought about the future the boy spoke of. But for Mack, the future was like a planet three jumps away, it might as well not exist for all it affected them. If Mack didn't freeze to death on the streets then things were going well. Through that lens, their life was full of blessings and this pod was heaven. In the morning Mack would have another go at searching apartments... and maybe buy two fried rats instead of a pod with noise proofing.

***

Mack woke up to the sound of hovercars honking outside their window and smiled. They rolled off the plush bed and realized the other side was empty. Sophia, who'd stayed the night, must have gone to get breakfast or just disappeared in general. It didn't bother Mack either way and they walked into the apartment's private auto-cleaner to get ready for the day. Mack felt like wearing something pretty today and picked out an expensive shirt with frills on it.

Working for Mr. Louise paid off in plenty of ways. Life here in the penthouses was a far cry from Mack's childhood on the streets. Now that Mr. Louise had passed, business was booming. Mack was still unlicensed, although multiple fake registration cards in the past dozen years would refute that claim. At this point, it was a game to see how long they could last without one.

Wandering out of the bedroom of the penthouse and into the kitchen they figured out where the girl from last night had wandered off to. She was wearing one of Mack's old shirts that said something in Common Tongue they couldn't read.

Sophia was thin as a skewer and the shirt draped over her like a nightgown. She smiled as Mack entered the room. With a hand intricately tattooed with white geometric patterns she presented Mack a plate of warm waffles.

"These are fluffier than usual," they said after taking a bite.

"These were made from scratch." Batter hissed as Sophia poured it into a metal sandwich-like machine. "Not just popped from freezer to toaster."

"You can do that?!" Mack asked. The kitchen of their apartment was for the chef, or cute guests, to use. Mack's job was to get into trouble and make sure the Badges didn't stick their noses in too deep.

"The flour you've got is the nicest I've ever seen," Sophia said gesturing to the pantry, "definitely didn't come from the vats here."

"Flowers shouldn't be in a closet," Mack said with a smile. Sophia indulged them with a laugh but it was cut off by an explosion at the door.

Not this again, Mack thought as smoke began to fill the room. If Mack knew they'd be dealing with Badges today their shirt would have fewer frills. Sophia coughed through the smoke while Mack wet a napkin with juice and put it over their nose and mouth. Their eyes would start stinging soon but Mack wanted to know which brute needed to be fired for this intrusion.

The Badges shouted something upon entering. They were clad in gas masks and body armor, but no visible 'hances. One appeared from the smoke in front of Mack and said some nonsense about them being under arrest. Mack lifted their free hand, they were too old and wise to resist or run. Mr. Louise taught them it was better to get lawyers involved to navigate these matters. But instead of cuffs, the Badge swung a club into their gut.

The blow shocked and stung at the same time. The person was using a sedater, a savage tool that combined a nightstick with an electric stun gun.

Badges from the Valley didn't have that in their arsenal. Mack knew this because it took years to smuggle them in for their own crew.

These aren't your average Badges. This ain't going to be cheap, Mack thought as they passed out.

***

Two black eyes, a dislocated shoulder, and at least one broken rib later Gideon the lawyer finally arrived. Mack was still cuffed to the table and there wasn't a launder in the Central System capable of getting this mess of blood out of their top.

Gideon explained Sophia was being charged with prostitution, which Mack was unsurprised by. It didn't take a top detective to realize a girl from the bottom of the Valley didn't legitimately earn a suite a dozen levels up. It did take a lazy accountant to make it easy for them to prove it and Mack wondered if the bean counter really needed both his kneecaps. Gideon assured them he'd work it out. Sophia might not get to keep the suite but that was just more reason for Mack to have her and her waffles over more often.

"The allegations against you are a bit more serious," Gideon explained. "I don't know if I'm going to be able to get you out of this."

"We own half the Badges here and have files on the rest of them," Mack said.

"These aren't your typical Badges."

Between the sedater and the brute in here interrogating Mack with his fist, Gideon was merely confirming their fear. "It's a Minister?"

"They sent him in from the Central System itself. Even the local law didn't know he was working here."

Ministers were high-level arbiters that worked directly for the Elders of the Central System. If he was willing to bring Mack in it was serious.

"We've got Chief Simon working on something but-"

"but he's going to want free shipments for the next solar cycle," Mack finished with the request the chief always made.

"Lifetime."

Mack scoffed, "That's going to be expensive." But they agreed. There was a way to make a lifetime supply of something only need to pay out for a few solar cycles.

"You need anything else?" Gideon asked, then added, "Aside from a decent doctor."

"I want to see that bastard of a Minister," Mack said. "The least he can do is read my charges to my face."

***

Gideon delivered on the request but the minister took his time arriving. Mack's stomach growled, the bite of waffles was the only food they'd gotten all day. The minister finally entered wearing the clean robes of his position. He casually sat down across from Mack. His jaw was soft and he sported a thin beard of light hair.

"We're charging you with three counts of smuggling in foreign agricultural products," he said placing a hand terminal in front of them to review.

Ignoring the terminal, Mack squinted at the man wondering if he was a Badge they'd gotten fired. If so this was an elaborate plot for revenge. "You grow up here?" they asked.

"Mater of fact I did. Mid-level. It was people like you and Mr. Derick Louise that always caused our family trouble."

Mack shrugged, "You know I ain't your problem. You can't prove I'm smuggling anything more dangerous than a peanut."

"There are proper channels for these things," he said.

"Your proper channels never did anything for anyone. People are starving in the streets without money or food," Mack shouted.

The minister stayed cool, "We have scholarships and apprenticeships to help those people out."

They scoffed knowing the quality of those programs. Mr. Louise had done more good offering people like Mack work than an apprenticeship ever could.

He began reading the summary of their charges followed by a lecture about how Galleria Valley's local flora could be harmed by imported plants and Mack wanted to make a quip about how people were harmed by lack of imported plants but thought it'd be too close to an admission for Gideon's liking.

Finally, the minister concluded his lecture with, "There's no future in a life of crime."

Mack shrugged, there'd never been much of a future for them anyway. They rattled the chains of their cuffs, "These are a bit uncomfortable, I ain't much of a runner and you've got enough Badges here to catch me if I decide to start that hobby."

"I don't think you're going to be a free person anytime soon."

The door of the room beeped and Gideon walked in. He put a hand terminal on the table for the minister to review. "Everything you're charging Mx. Mack for has legitimate paperwork."

The minister reviewed the files his eyebrows wrinkled like a brooding storm.

"I don't know where you're getting your information but your records must be incomplete," Gideon continued. "Now please release my client."

The minister cursed the Elders he was so faithful to and checked his terminal. Mack let a small smile grow across their face. Mr. Louise had always said corruption ran stem to stern. Like rats, it followed humanity to every planet they colonized.

Mack always made the most of a good rat.

Unringing the Bell

M y troubles began when the test results popped up in front of my eyes. A remarkable 330 points on the ASLAN screener was good. It was great. Too great. I'd never expected to do that well. I didn't understand what doors it would open. What doors I'd be dragged through because of it.

I sat, reclined, in a high-backed silver lesson chair. The black pads embedded in the seat did the bare minimum to cushion my back and bum. The blue holoscreen hovered centimeters from my eye displaying the homework I was supposed to be working on. The nodes of the neural cap were connected to my scalp with slick gel that I always hated. It deflated the big curls of my hair that I spent all morning putting in.

Why wake up three hours early just to do my hair and makeup if it'll be ruined an hour into class?

Every teenager rebels in her own way.

I only had to use the stupid neural cap because I didn't have a microfuser yet. Most of the boys in the class had one installed by now. Metal computers inset around their left eyes. Lights flashed on their occipital bone as you talked with them and you wondered what they were doing on those little computers imbedded in their mind.

It was important they got them early. Important that they familiarize themselves with the tech. As future execs, they'd need to be comfortable running at full capacity without overclocking.

Most girls didn't have one yet. Some hoped they'd never get one. They wanted to look beautiful and unmarred, like their mothers. Wanted to marry rich execs like their fathers.

I wanted two microfusers just to spite my grandfather. He'd refused to approve the installation on his granddaughter. What silly dreams I had.

If only I'd known what I'd become.

I can remember the classroom crystal clearly. I could calculate the number of hairs on the back of Joey Ritvala's head right now if I had to. Simulate the whole experience as if I were there. It'd be simple with the amount of memory space I have now. Wouldn't strain my processors at all.

The 42 lesson chairs were arranged into six neat rows. Wires that ran from the floor were bundled neatly with cable ties. Reprinted art by archaic artists hung on the walls. Abstract swaths of primary colors in the shape of animals I'd only ever read about or eaten.

Clouds loomed outside the high tower window. A breeze made their wisps swirl lightly. It was another rainy day in the Valley. Luckily I wouldn't have to go out and get wet.

I should've jumped out the window then and there.

Mr. Chaler, my Contracts teacher, sat in front of the class in his lecture chair, a bigger, and slightly more comfortable version of our lesson chairs. He was young, just out of school a few years ago. His curly black hair was cut in a neat high and tight style. There were 94,256 hairs on his head. 56,489 curled in a counterclockwise direction. He had 9 pimples on his forehead and cheeks, with 6 more emerging.

Of course, I didn't recognize any of this at the time. Wish I didn't notice it now. I'd be better off ignoring it. The details don't bring me comfort.

Mr. Chaler's microfuser was wired into the armrest of his lecture chair. A silver flatworm cable slinked down his arm connecting him to the rest of the class. Enabling him to monitor our work, answer our questions, and send us lecture notes.

Which meant he saw everything on our screens.

Which means he saw my score.

"Congratulations to Ms. Pascuzzo for her remarkable score on the ASLAN screener!" He announced to the class. His voice transmitted through our headsets despite him being close enough that we could hear him speak. It was the familiar lecture echoing that all students in the Valley were familiar with.

My cheeks flushed red at the few students who cared enough to look at me.

Cherie Salman was one of them, her microfuser around her eye flashed lights. "No one ever thought you'd be the reason Chaler gets his semester bonus," she said. Her lips twisted into a thin grin. She hadn't transmitted them electronically but the comment was loud enough for the whole class to hear.

"Now now, it's not just about the bonus. I teach all of you because it's how I contribute to Baumein's future as a company."

"And because your other option was being a butchered manti," Joey Ritvala transmitted.

His comment was immediately censored on the lecture's conversation record. Not that teachers hadn't reminded us of the consequences of not excelling in school, or in the company. Kid's opinions didn't form in a vacuum.

But company policy was that manticores did important work on the docks, even if 80% of them were also smuggling for mobsters. And inaccurate slurs like "manti" were unacceptable on official records.

"Good job," Robert Spencer said to me from the lecture chair nearby. He was one of the few boys who hadn't gotten a microfuser yet. A few other kids transmitted their congratulations over the classroom's network.

They were all interrupted when Headmaster Unreine walked into the classroom. His hard-soled shoes clicked and clacked with every step. A staccato sound sure to cut all but the most delinquent students off. And Crest Tower Academy did not tolerate delinquent students.

Unreine was a tin man, there wasn't a single superficial part of him that wasn't enhanced. Some kids said he even replaced his heart during the War of Acquisition. His infamous strictness was all the evidence they needed to validate that rumor.

He wore a black suit, black tie, and white button-up undershirt. Same thing every man employed by Baumein wore. Girls got the option to wear a skirt. The choices we made influenced how the world saw us and what path we intended to take. Exec, or exec's wife. Some of us changed our preferences daily, just to keep everyone guessing.

"Ms. Bellina," the headmaster said in the synthesized voice of his electronic vocal cords. He could shout across a hallway without strain if need be. He could weaponize it and make ears bleed if he had to.

"I'm sure Mr. Chaler has already congratulated you on your remarkable score," Unreine said. "I would also like to praise you for such an accomplishment."

Everyone in the classroom knew he'd be getting a bonus for my performance as well. Even if he hadn't passed me a second glance up to this point.

"Please come with me to my office so we can discuss your future."

The holoscreen in front of me shut down without my command. I didn't want to join the headmaster in his office, I didn't want to discuss my future. I still had two more years in this corporate school. Dances to attend, school council elections to win, and a few yearbooks to assemble. After all that I would decide what kind of career I wanted to pursue.

With my scores on the test and my father's executive position, there was no doubt I could request just about any position in the conglomerate. Whether or not I had the political power to keep it was another story. Hence the importance of my participation on the school council and yearbook committee.

But the headmaster's tone gave me no room to argue. I couldn't get the holoscreen to display my homework as much as I wanted to. I pulled the neural cap off my head and did my best to readjust my slick hair.

I followed the headmaster down the narrow hallways of the schools back to his office. The halls were desolate between classes. Metal lockers that opened with biometric logins covered the walls in uniform navy blue. Screens embedded above them had sine wave screensavers, during passing period they'd be replaced with loud school spirit campaigns and ads for products Baumein wanted to be popular with teens.

The ASLAN screener I'd done so well on was an aptitude test. Nothing remarkable, I'd taken a half dozen up to this point. Hadn't done particularly remarkable on any of them. So how I jumped up in scores was surprising to me... at the time.

In the headmaster's office, I sat across from Mr. Unreine in a plastic navy blue chair. His black sheet metal desk with a faux wood top was covered in 17 glass tablets, an 81-centimeter monitor, nine contraband cigarettes (one of which belonged to no manufacturer I'm currently aware of leading me to believe it was homemade), and a wooden plaque with his name carved into it. Even at the time, I doubted it'd been carved by hand or that it was genuine wood.

"With your scores, you've qualified to be a towermind," the headmaster informed me.

I shrugged leaned back in the chair, crossed my legs, and made sure my skirt fell politely just past my knees. I wasn't interested in being a towermind. Who would be?

"It will be a large responsibility and a demanding position but Crest Tower Academy has taught you everything you need to know to excel in your new position."

"I'm not interested in being a towermind," I stated it flat and firm, like my dad had taught me when we practiced negotiating for dessert.

"Oh," his metal eyebrows went high on his chrome forehead to feign shock since his voice box couldn't. "Our pre-test records indicate that you agreed to take the position of towermind as soon as possible based on the results of the ASLAN screener."

Headmaster Unreine turned his monitor to face me since he couldn't transmit the electronic document to a holoscreen in front of my eyes.

"Additionally, all of your application paperwork for this academy and paperwork going back to the first grade indicates you were willing to take on this important role. And of course, this is an honorable position for the Baumein conglomerate."

I scrolled through the paperwork, there were always digital reams of this stuff to sign before a test or new school year. If you actually read it all there'd be no time to take the test.

Unfortunately, I'd signed to agree to be a towermind. But under that agreement, I'd signed to be a tower repair agent, then a transmission specialist, and a dozen other jobs all alphabetically listed.

"It's the first time I'm hearing that you're not interested in this towermind role," Unreine continued. "And of course, I of all people understand hesitation to incorporate new enhancements into your life." His metal lips smiled with the whir of servos under his shell. He picked up a Vestige brand cigarette, it looked like a pen with a mouthpiece on the end and twirled it between his metal fingers. "I assure you, your enhancements will not be noticed, nor would will you regret the decision."

He was incorrect on both counts.

"I had to sign all this to get into the school or take these tests and pass the school year. I didn't actually think it would come to anything."

"Well, that's the whole point of your contracts class that Mr. Chaler is teaching. To understand how important and binding all these agreements we have to sign every day are. They hold up the fabric of our conglomerate. Dare I go so far to say they hold the very towers we live in up. They make the Valley the luscious place it is."

I doubted he'd gone any lower in the building than this school's floor. Likely spent most of his time in his penthouse and whatever luxuries it provided.

"I didn't have a choice to not sign these," I protested.

"Oh course you did," and his voice box made an inhuman chuckle that was more similar to an amateur violin player than an actual laugh. "You could have withdrawn from the school and taken lessons elsewhere. It is a free market after all."

He was right. We could study anywhere we wanted. Other academies in other towers which had just as many contracts to sign, or complete the public seminars, online pre-recorded lectures that were outdated and the degree approved you to do data entry at best. The connections to other future executives at high-tower academies like this one were necessary for success in a conglomerate like Baumein.

"Well, don't I still need to graduate? I still have a few years until I'll be eligible for employment."

"There's a towermind position currently open. Which is why we gave the ASLAN screener off-cycle. The position needs to be filled immediately. And Crest Tower Academy is proud to be able to contribute one of their alumni."

"I don't want this!" I stomped my foot down on the ground. The soft rubber sole of my Mary Jane flat barely made a sound. "I won't do it. You can't make me."

Headmaster Unreine scrolled down on the contract on his monitor to show me more fine print I was uninterested in reading when I first signed it, and now. "You're correct, nothing can force you to work as a towermind however a breach of these contracts can lead to long-term ineligibility of employment for you and your family." His synthetic voice was emotionless despite the sinister threat.

Ineligibility of employment could limit my sister's education. It could theoretically limit my father's executive position, but he and my grandfather had so many accolades I couldn't imagine that happening. And it certainly wouldn't affect Grandpa, he was a high executive, untouchable by anyone but the board. He would know how to lobby against this decision.

"I'll rebel! I'll shut down the tower if you make me a mind!" I stood up with my protest and pushed my deflated brown curls out of my eyes. I wasn't interested in contracts or employment or anything.

"You won't be able to. You'll be programmed not to rebel, or even care about being a towermind. It's for the safety of everyone."

I groaned in frustration and stormed out of the office. I expected to hear Unreine's commanding voice tell me to stop, or the click-clack of his shoes to follow me to the door. But neither came.

I could feel tears forming in my eyes. Crying in a negotiation was a move I'd abandoned ages ago, at least I thought I had. My mind, more occupied by what was behind me than in front of me, ran into someone's black slacks.

I looked up to see my father dressed in his business suit. Despite his olive skin he still looked too similar to Unreine for my comfort. My mother stood next to him distracted by the hand terminal she had to use since she did not have a microfuser installed.

"Congratulations on your ASLAN score," my father said. "We're here to discuss it with your headmaster. We're all quite proud of you."

"I don't want to be a towermind. I just want to go back to class!" I pushed back tears that welled in my eyes. I still have to push them back today despite them being imperceptible in this vat.

"I'm sure we can work something out," my father said. He directed me to a chair outside the office. It was the same navy plastic blue kind that sat across from Unreine's desk. I sat in it hesitantly.

My parents disappeared behind the office door, frosted glass hid everything but the form of their black jackets.

"Sour gum?" A boy next to me said.

I wiped the tears from my eyes. Tried not to sniffle. Failed.

Robert Spencer sat next to me, holding out a stick of gum wrapped in tin foil.

I unwrapped the foil, it was creased in eight places to hold the stick of gum in place. As soon as the gum hit my tongue my eyes squinted and my lips puckered. It was intense enough to take my mind off my problems, if only for a moment.

"What are you doing here?" I asked Robert after I'd chewed enough of the gum to release the sweet fruity flavor that always followed the sour acidity.

"Supposed to meet with the counselor but he's still out at lunch." Robert popped his gum loudly against his teeth gaining both of us a glare from the woman at the front desk.

Robert was a good kid, not a troublemaker or a bully. I didn't know him well. Knew he had some trouble at home recently but that hadn't been big enough gossip to spread the details to my ears.

"What does the counselor want to talk to you about?" I asked.

"I'm a ward of the company since my mom died. Mr. Schmeek wants to talk to me about getting a microfuser to improve my grades and increase the difficulties of my classes."

"Oh," I wished gossip had spread a little further then I wouldn't have pried so deep. "Sorry about your mom."

Robert shrugged, popped his gum a few more times while looking directly at the woman at the front desk who groaned and rolled her eyes.

"I don't want to get a microfuser." He sounded scared and small. "But my ASLAN scores were low and Mr. Schmeek says if this quarter of school doesn't go well for me I'll be out on the streets."

"A microfuser can't be that bad. Basically, everyone has one," I said. I sensed it was the wrong thing to say as Robert frowned. "But I get not wanting one. They want to make me a towermind because of my scores, so be glad you didn't do that well."

Robert shivered in his seat as if I'd told him a ghost story. "You're not going to do it though. Right?"

"I don't plan to," I said defiantly. "But they've got contracts with my signature. The ones we had to sign to take the test."

Robert sighed. "Contracts are the reason I'm sleeping at the boy's dorm instead of living with my father in High Tower."

"High Tower's Mandlestadt. I didn't know—"

"Neither did I. Until he came to pick me up. But the dorm's prefect wouldn't let him take me, said I was still committed to contributing to the Baumein conglomerate. I thought the prefect wanted to me stay so he wouldn't have to pick up my chores. But Schmeek showed me the paperwork. I'm theirs... until I flunk out."

"Then you can go be with your dad," I said. Hopeful. Even if he was a Mandlestadt it'd be better than being on the streets.

"They won't want me with my grade—"

"My daughter will not be turned into a computer just because of some compulsory contracts," my father shouted. The volume of his synthetic vocal cords, a nicer set than Unreine's, shook the glass of the office but still carried a sense of compassion for me. At least that's what I always tell myself I heard.

"You will not ruin my bonus," Unreine had raised his voice as well but the tinny synthetic chords made him sound berserk. "Nor will you sully the prestigiousness of this school's ASLAN accomplishments. Removing her from the candidate pool would show a lack of willingness to contribute to Baumein's mission."

My mother rushed out of the room covering her ears and slamming the door behind her to muffle the sound, if only a little. My father's electric eardrums could handle the abuse.

"You will not—cannot—question my family's loyalty to Baumein. Our commitment spans generations to before the war. Nullify those contracts or your next promotion will be so low in the tower you'll smell street sewage."

I always knew my family was important. At dinners, Grandpa would tell us his father's stories from the War of Acquisition. He reminded all his grandchildren that one day they'd be responsible for much more than just cleaning their room and acing homework assignments.

My father inherited his executive position from my grandfather after an early promotion. I'd heard about our family's weight being used in negotiations. But seeing it happen on my own behalf, I thought it might just get me out of this contract.

"These contracts are sealed tighter than the dock's seawall," Unreine announced. "Not even a board member could get out of them. They're designed to protect Baumein's future," Unreine lowered his voice from a shout to an announcer's level. "You're not the first parent to be upset by them. But it will pass, as it does with all parents. When you understand the criticality of Ms. Bellina's contribution."

My father groaned at full volume. It shattered the frosted glass window of Unreine's office but not a single bolt was rattled in the tin man. The servos of his metal lips held fast in a shallow but smug grin.

My father stormed out of the room, his heavy-soled shoes clomping on the ground with every step. "Come on Bell," he said and reached out for my hand. "You're no longer enrolled here." His voice was above a conversational tone, but it wasn't a shout. My mother followed, still massaging her ear.

"These are not flimsy corporate contracts you can weasel out of to fatten up your bottom line," Unreine said from behind us.

The taunt was emotionless but loomed behind us as we left the office and the school.

***

I sat at the long glass conference table in a high-backed office chair that felt like it was swallowing me up. My father sat across from me. He argued with my grandfather who was sitting next to me at the head of the table. It wasn't an outright shouting match but the subtle cutting words they traded made everyone in the room feel uncomfortable. We had a few options on what would happen next with me, none of which were good.

I felt like I had more in common with the conference table than either of the execs discussing my future.

The elevator ride up to Grandfather's penthouse was more tense and quiet than the time I'd gotten caught making out with Taylor McFee in the library. It wasn't the act itself that'd gotten me in trouble, it was getting caught that was the problem for my parents.

This incident felt similar in more ways than one.

Grandfather's assistant, Mr. Pumpernickle looked into the contract as soon as my father called him. We hadn't left the school yet and my father was subvocalizing the situation through his microfuser. My mother was clicking on the touchscreen of her hand terminal with a purpose I'd only seen once before when she was running behind on the Winter Gala plans.

I walked through the heavy bulletproof doors of the meeting room. A small squadron of lawyers and associates sat around the glass conference room table wearing their cookie-cutter black suits. They were loyal to my grandfather, and family, due to ties from and in some cases before the War of Acquisition.

My grandfather stood up from his seat at the head of the table to greet me. Everyone else at the table followed his lead.

My school contracts were presented on the various screens that hung on the walls of the room. One was behind my grandfather, two more flanked the table so that he could see what data appeared behind him.

I had only been in the conference room three times. It was not a place for children. So of course my cousins and I snuck in during a busy party my grandparents hosted, twice. The third time was when my father got his promotion to executive. It was a shame that the tension of negotiating my contracts ruined the elation I held for the room.

Grandfather offered the seat next to him and Pumpernickel moved to his right, causing a chain reaction of seat migration down the entire length of the table. Grandfather reassured me that we would figure this out and that I would not be employed in such an undignified role. His long silver hair swept to one side and his comforting smile that created 8 symmetrical wrinkles around his mouth and eyes made me feel like we'd figure something out.

Five hours later, with no break for dinner, and that reassurance was waning.

After spending the better part of an afternoon and evening with the lawyers I realized they were slightly more diverse than the suits implied. Two of them were tin men like my headmaster. I was glad they were seated far from me at the foot of the table. It was only later that I realized they were security detail, not certified lawyers.

Young lawyers, whose grandfathers had fought beside my great-grandfather in the War of Acquisition, threw out ideas left and right. Each had a microfuser, a few had 'hanced hands or arms that bulged subtly against the suit. One woman stood out to me as she had dual microfusers around her eyes.

Most of the ideas this young group proposed were rudimentary loopholes you could find in a typical contract where either party wanted an escape route. My academy had left no loopholes.

The senior lawyers, who sat near my parents and Mr. Pumpernickel, quickly shot down these suggestions as they found the terms that eliminated these approaches. The senior lawyers, some so old they'd served directly under my great-grandfather in the war, were well connected enough to formulate a plan to get me out of the Baumein conglomerate altogether.

Which was exactly what my father and grandfather were arguing about.

No one had proposed the obvious. The young associates were likely too scared to voice it. The elders were likely too steadfast with honor to consider it. Over the past few hours, I'd felt both ways.

I interjected myself into the executive's conversation using the firmest adult voice my unenhanced vocal cords could muster.

"Why don't I just become a towermind and everyone else can go along with their lives?"

My father and grandfather looked at me then at each other. They didn't have the shock of someone who hadn't considered the option. Instead, they seemed confused by whether or not I was serious.

"You do not want to be a towermind, Ms. Bellina," Pumpernickel said in the same voice he used to tell us stories before bed when my parents worked late and the nanny needed to get home to her own kids. "You'll be wired into a building, responsible for all the central computing it does. Unable to leave the basement where you're connected."

"I know."

I did not know.

To this day I am unsure if Pumpernickel knew the truth and hid it or was ignorant of the towermind process.

"But I've agreed to these contracts," I continued. "I'd rather continue to serve Baumein than be smuggled into musty a Mandlestadt tower."

Pumpernickel let out a light chuckle that could only be made by biological vocal cords and looked at my grandfather.

"The school has done a good job teaching you Baumein propaganda. But Pascuzzos do not hold contracts that are not in their best interest," Grandfather said. "Baumein didn't come out on top during the war by complying with unfavorable terms. This family will maintain the respect it's earned. It will not be tarnished by the eldest of your generation becoming a glorified computer."

"Mr. Pascuzzo I've found the information on the next highest ASLAN score," The dual microfuser lawyer interjected. She spoke quickly, her mind operating at the hyper speed of her microfusers. She'd respectfully turned to address my grandfather but her eyes focused past him at whatever data was projected over them.

The profile of a soft-chinned teenage boy who I'd never met but looked just like the many future executives I attended class with appeared on the screens around the room. Jason Liesel, lived on level 34 D of Pinemark Tower, far across the Valley. He wasn't from a particularly prestigious family. His mother was an associate and his father was a minor executive.

"His score is ten percentile lower and would be a viable towermind candidate," the associate continued, speaking almost faster than I could understand.

"Wonderful, his parents should be easy to negotiate with," my father said. He spoke quickly as well, navigating something on his own microfuser. "The boy's father has an honest enough employment history it won't be hard to get him a promotion. Any siblings?"

"No sir," Mr. Pumpernickel replied.

"I'll make sure the promotion is lucrative enough that his wife can retire and they'll have time for more kids," my grandfather said.

"Wait we're just putting him in a situation worse than my own," I interjected. "That's not fair. Wouldn't his family do the same as us if they had loyal lawyers like us?"

Most of the associates didn't seem to register my remark, they were busy organizing a promotion package for the father of this boy.

"Nothing in the Valley is fair," my mother said soft and slow. "This family has earned special privileges because of your great-grandfather's service in the war."

"Our delivery bot reports Mr. Liesel has opened the promotional offer," a senior lawyer reported.

"Mr. Pascuzzo, have you reviewed Ms. Bellina's scheduled posting?" Pumpernickel asked facing my grandfather. He spoke slowly despite his eyes being glazed over from using his microfuser.

"I have not dignified it with my attention." My grandfather spat the words out quickly.

"I believe it would inform our decisions if you did." Mr. Pumpernickel was firm but still cordial. "I've sent them to you directly."

"Put it on the screens," my grandfather said. "Get Mr. Liesel on a call," he ordered a young associate. "Or send a car to get him here if need be. I don't want him to even consider declining us."

"I think it would be best if you reviewed them in private," Mr. Pumpernickel said.

The room fell so quiet that the servos of the tin men's shocked expressions could be heard from the edge of the table. If any other non-family member in that room had made a comment second-guessing my grandfather that directly they would've been escorted from the penthouse and immediately demoted.

My grandfather slowed down his speaking either to emphasize his point and make sure I understood. "My eldest granddaughter will be aware of every byte of information this counsel is privy to. This is not only a family emergency but a remarkable learning opportunity for a future executive. And while her solutions and perspectives may be naive that will not be fixed by censoring information."

"Yes sir," Pumpernickel replied.

The boy's image and profile were removed from the screen. Encrypted data was unpacked, and more levels of encryption were hacked through than I'd ever imagined up to that point in my life. The job description for my towermind position hovered just over my grandfather's head on the wall.

It was a top-secret project based in Spiegel Tower. The tower was infamous. Instead of being built like a column it was a tall pyramid. Every window of the building was polished like a mirror, it often reflected the clouds that covered the Valley.

The project was unspecified, even in this top secret of a document. But the score required of the towermind was not. I'd beaten the score by 30 points. Jason, at ten percent below me, fell just short of the qualifying mark.

"Doctor the boy's score," my grandfather immediately proposed. "He only needs three points to qualify."

The room remained silent.

My father spoke up. "These are board member-certified tests. This project is directly serving Board Member Hoffmann."

My father did not have to explain that going against a board member so directly would be career suicide for even our family.

"It explains why the headmaster wouldn't take a bribe," my grandfather muttered. "The compensation bonus for the tin man filling this position would set him up for another hundred years of 'hance maintenance. Sewage and seawater, another century as a teacher, can't fathom why anyone would want it."

The room was at an impasse. Unwilling to comply with my grandfather's previous directive for fear of upsetting a board member. Unable to propose anything new for fear of upsetting my grandfather.

With growling stomachs, we waited for my grandfather to give his next instruction.

"Very well," he finally broke the silence. His eyes focused on me and the others in the room, no longer distracted by his microfuser. He spoke in a measured tone so no one would misunderstand his instruction. "Bellina will need to die and be smuggled to a Mandlestadt tower."

While my death would only be on paper, to him it was the equivalency of pruning a vibrant flowering branch of the family tree forever.

"You'll place her with nothing less than a senior executive family," he continued. "They may be Mandlestadts but I want Bell not to lose all her culture."

***

The sewers smelled worse than I'd ever imagined. The sulfur smell reminded me of a chemistry lab class I took the previous semester. Thick greenish-brown sewage came up to my knee. Luckily I wore rubber overalls that insulated me from the ooze.

I could taste the hollandaise sauce from dinner at the back of my throat. It'd topped a filet of salmon and fresh broccolini and was probably my last meal on paper since some associate was filing a death certificate while I ate.

The two tin men from the meeting led the pack with Mr. Pumpernickel behind them. The assistant looked strange not wearing his black suit. I'd only seen him out of it a handful of times, each event more unexpected and abnormal than the last.

Right now he wore the same overalls as me. Crest Tower Waste Management was stenciled on the back in fading black letters. The black t-shirt he wore under it exposed his 'hanced arms.

I knew his arms were 'hanced; his silver hands were visible even under a suit. Plus I always enjoyed when he'd effortlessly throw me meters into the air as a kid. I giggled uncontrollably the whole time.

What I hadn't known was that there were seven dents from bullet holes, five unpolished scratches, and one missing panel on his left bicep where you could see the inner workings of the arm as it moved. I hadn't taken the time to count all the dings in the sewer but as the memory replays, I have no problem recounting the details.

The arms weren't in disrepair due to financial need. My grandfather surely paid him well. But Pumpernickel had always been sentimental, loyal, and good at keeping things out of the recycler even if that's where they belonged. I just never expected that to apply to his own arms.

Once as a child I threw a fit to my nanny about my stuffed elephant no longer playing a trumpeting fanfare when I hugged it. Pumpernickel disappeared with it for a day or two. My parents replaced the toy with a newer nicer stuffed animatronic elephant that balanced a ball on its nose.

It wasn't the same. A week later Pumpernickel returned with the old elephant repaired and able to play the tune again. The only difference was the big patch on the elephant's tummy that I didn't mind.

Even if he was a great repair man it was a mystery to me how he might go about repairing his own arms. But maybe it was a case of the best hairdresser at a salon having the worst haircut.

My grandfather walked beside me. One hand clutched a flashlight-shaped object that was currently powered down. The other hand occasionally reached out to catch me when I slipped on flotsam that settled under the ooze.

Occasionally my foot would crush whatever I stepped on. The rubber soles of the overalls let me feel what was underneath. The worst feeling was stepping on something squishy settling on what felt like a pipe then hearing and feeling it snap underneath.

At the time I blocked out what that could have been. It is no secret that bodies disappear into the sewer for gutter service funerals. Now, with countless processors at my disposal, I have no doubt I stepped on a limb. Whether it was amputated to be replaced by bionics or still attached to a body I'll never know. But there's no doubt that it'd been decomposing in the ooze of the sewage for three to four weeks.

Father walked behind me with my mother, who insisted on coming along to see me off. Whether or not this stinky send-off was the way she'd imagined it was never clear. Nonetheless, I was, and am, glad she came.

Father kept telling her to slide her feet across the surface instead of picking them up. It was a motion that felt strange to me. My mother had difficulty with it. To everyone else in the group, it seemed fairly natural.

"Just slide you—" my father started again. The clink of Pumpernickel's fingers clenching in a fist against his palm shut him up.

The tin men, no overalls since the ooze didn't bother their 'hanced legs, unfolded their arms into assault rifles. Looking past Pumpernickel I saw a light coming down a bend in the sewage piping we stood inside.

My grandfather pushed me closer to Pumpernickel and held the object in his hand like the hilt it was. The laser sword was used by my great-grandfather during the war. Now it was brought out of storage for this occasion.

My father stood in front of my mother, his slender 'hanced left arm ready to draw the gun buried under his arm in a shoulder holster. This Mandlestadt meeting was with a trusted contact but there was still plenty of risk when transacting business with a competitor.

The group turned the corner, their blinding headlamps shone in our faces.

"Are you the representatives for Mr. Arakida?" Pumpernickel called out down the sewer. It was the loudest any of us had spoken in the past half hour of travel and the sound echoed uncomfortably through the sewer pipe.

"Yeah. You?"

"Nikandr Pugachyov. We spoke over the phone," Pumpernickel replied.

The Mandlestadts dimmed their lights making it easier to make out the three figures in front of us. A woman with broad 'hanced shoulders and arms had two slender men standing behind her. The man on my right did the negotiations with Pumpernickel as my family watched intently, at least a little at ease by the fact they brought half the manpower we did.

They may be doing my grandfather a favor for hiding me, but they weren't getting a ward as valuable as me for nothing. These Mandlestadt associates, lower-level representatives for a Mandlestadt exec, provided Pumpernickel with a cyberton of insider information. Including intimate information about the executive who would soon become my guardian. Blackmail was better protection than any contract.

"Bell will be tutored by Mrs. Hanako, correct?" My mom asked nervously.

The man negotiating with Pumpernickel seemed confused. So did everyone else in our group.

"Bell is going to need help in math. I know Mrs. Hanako is the tutor who works for your executive Mr. Arakida."

"Yes, yes, of course. All of Ms. Pascuzzo's teaching needs will be taken care of," the representative said.

Before he could turn back to look at Pumpernickel my mother interjected again. "And Chef Mari knows that she is allergic to fish?"

I was not allergic to fish and I almost interjected but my father beat me to it.

"Bell isn't—"

"Please, dear. I want to make sure our daughter is taken care of." My mother spoke in a tone a voice that was not only dismissive of my father's comment but seemed genuinely intrigued by the representative's response.

"Chef Mari takes into account everyone's dietary needs. You have nothing to worry about Ms. Pascuzzo will be in good hands."

"Wonderful," my mother said. The tone reminded me of all the times I'd picked out a dress for a gala only to find it missing come the day of the event. Of course, the dress my mother actually wanted me to wear was neatly set out for me with matching jewelry to go with it.

She pulled out her hand terminal as Pumpernickel went back to work transacting data under the watchful eye of my grandfather.

The LED lights of my grandfather's microfuser flashed in time with my father's and Pumpernickel's. It would've been imperceptible if the sewers weren't so dark.

It happened in a flash but the events can easily be slowed down in my memory to the point of being able to simulate all the different currents and ripples in the stagnant sewage water.

My father's gun exited his holster a half second after my grandfather's sword came to life. The bright white glow was blinding in the dark and it was likely the only reason my father's first shot missed the man transacting data with Pumpernickel.

Pumpernickel, unfazed by the bullet flying past his ear was able to duck down and pull me out of the way of the fight. He bundled me in his silver arms and took three long strides to the edge of the sewer.

My grandfather took two steps forward swung the sword at the metal arm of the woman and sliced through her mid forearm. The laser was designed to cut through enhanced limbs like butter. Hydraulic fluid spurted out of the wound and mixed in with the sewage under us.

I didn't recognize it at the time but neither of the tin men made a move. They should've at least immobilized the Mandlestadt reps but they merely stood like well-armed statues.

They should've stopped the third Mandlestadt rep from drawing his gun and firing it at my mother. It hit her just below the ribs. She fell down to a knee and clutched her side. I expected to see horror in her eyes from being shot. Instead, she looked at me relieved to see me safe in Pumpernickel's grasp.

My father grabbed her with his right arm while his 'hanced one stayed trained on the reps. The shooter wasn't able to take a second shot as my grandfather decapitated him with a single swoop of the sword.

The smell of roasted holiday ham cut through the stench of the sewage if only for a moment. The man fell limp into the water the gentle current of the sewage carried his body away from the scuffle.

"Stop it," Pumpernickel said, his unenhanced voice was right next to my ear. The sound echoed through the sewer pipe. The command was firmer than I'd ever heard him speak before. This was no conference room negotiation.

"These men aren't in Mr. Arakida's employment. The chef and tutor were both fired three quarters ago," my father explained helping my mother up and letting her lean on his shoulder. The gyroscopes of his slender 'hanced arm kept his gun trained on the Mandlestadt representative no matter what his body did.

Mother hadn't fallen so much that sewage got in her overalls or the wound. Both of which would be dangerous if not fatal.

My grandfather was in no mood to discuss the situation, I believe the only reason he hadn't already used his sword on the other two was because he wanted answers from them.

"I know," Mr. Pumpernickel said. "But how did you find out?" He turned to look down at my mother who was leaning on my father at this point.

My father's flesh arm seemed strained to hold her up. The 'hanced one could handle it no problem, but it'd cost him the ability to accurately fire his gun, a payment he was not willing to make at this time.

I wanted to turn my head to look Pumpernickel in the face but one arm held held me close to his chest while his other hand rested on the nape of my neck. I was as immobile as the tin men.

"A mommy... group I'm a... part of," my mother coughed the words out slowly, "gave me information... about Arakida's house to verify... Bell's safety." She tried to stand up straight to face down Pumpernickel but the effort was too much. With a groan, her knees buckled and she leaned heavily on my father.

"You're behind this?" My grandfather said facing Pumpernickel the tip of his sword pointing at us nearly blinding me. Enhanced eyes would have no problem filtering the light of the sword out, they'd been designed to do it for generations. The best mine could do was squint.

"I am," Pumpernickel admitted. "And I'm sorry." His voice was warm but the metal hand on my neck was a stark contrast and made me doubt him. "Baumien was onto the transfer. They didn't believe the hastily filed death certificate. The best thing I could do for the family was help them intercept the trade-off."

"You're willing to let my granddaughter become a towermind for what? How handsome is this bonus they're paying you that it's worth risking your life?"

"You weren't supposed to know," Pumpernickel said.

"What's the bonus?" My grandfather repeated.

"Nothing," Pumpernickel replied.

My grandfather's expression was as still as stone. "Do not betray me and lie to me on the same day. You knew I could match whatever their price was."

"Board Member Hoffmann filed to make the entire house ineligible for employment if Ms. Pascuzzo didn't become a towermind."

"My family goes far enough back that we'd—"

"The entire house," Pumpernickel's voice waived as he explained. "Everyone you and your children employ from the nanny to the maids to the interns. Unemployable to Baumein. Relegated to the bottom of the Valley. Unfit for even a data entry job."

"You would've been fine, we would've taken care of you." My father said.

"But now you betray us," my grandfather growled. "There won't be a safe place in the entire Valley for you."

"I know," Pumpernickel said. "But your staff will be safe from the gangs of the Valley floor. But only if Bell and I leave now."

"Put her down," my father said. He shifted his left arm to point at Pumpernickel. The arm was precise enough that he could shoot Pumpernickel between the brow leaving me unscathed. "I won't let you take her."

Pumpernickel stretched his fingers out from around my neck and then rested them back. The threat was clear, his metal hands could snap my neck, crush my skull, pull me limb from limb. It wouldn't strain his servos in the slightest.

But it'd strain his heart. He wouldn't do it, I told myself. Just like my father wouldn't shoot the man who'd been such a close part of the family for decades.

My grandfather seemed to agree with my assumption Pumpernickel wouldn't do it but didn't have the reservations of my father. He stepped towards us and swiftly sliced at Pumpernickel's arm.

The heat of his sword singed the flesh of my shoulder. It burned through the rubber strap and cooked my flesh.

I hung in the air far from my grandfather's reach and Pumpernickel's chest. Pumpernickel had moved me out of the way in time to keep everything still attached to my body.

Pumpernickel was not so lucky.

His dismembered hand plunked into the sewage.

"Quit!" I said. I hung in the air, Pumpernickel's remaining hand had no problem holding me there. "I'm going with Pumpernickel."

It wasn't worth the jobs that would be lost over me. It wasn't worth the fight and injuries we'd sustained so far. I didn't know what being a towermind would cost but I knew it wasn't worth this.

I remind myself of this day, of this decision, of why I chose this life. Not because I'd signed a contract, but because if I didn't play by the rules of the Valley many more people would suffer.

My processors are occupied with this memory because it's more important than the elevators I schedule, and the simulations I run, and the accountants I help. In the sewers that night I chose to keep people out of the bottom of the Valley, for a day or a week. Hopefully longer.

"You don't know what you're getting yourself into," my father said. He was right.

"I don't care," I said. "Grandfather employs hundreds of people. If they and their family are wrapped up in this breach of contract it'll ruin countless lives. I'm not worth it."

"You are," my grandfather said. He used his negotiation voice, the statement was an immutable fact he was unwilling to compromise.

"Let her go," my mother said weakly. She pulled on my father encouraging him to listen to us. All the calculations he was able to do in his head. It couldn't do the simple math that my mother and I'd done without microfusers.

"Get mom to a hospital," I said, "let me go, granddad. It's what I want. It's for the best. Even your connections can't protect everyone in the house."

"I don't care about anyone else in the house but the family," he admitted.

"I do. And if you care about me you'll at least act like you care about them."

The white light of the laser sword shone bright against his face casting a shadow in the Valley of every one of his wrinkles. The lights of his microfuser flashed, I thought he'd make a move not caring about his life or Pumpernickels just wanting to get me free from the assistant's grasp.

When the lights of his microfuser turned off so did the sword.

"Go," he said.

The two remaining fake Mandlestadt associates rushed down the sewer making loud sloshing steps that echoed through the pipes.

"I'm sorry," Pumpernickel said as he backed away. His handless arm wrapped around my waist spilling hydraulic fluid on my rubber overalls

"Will the frozen tin men be okay?" I asked as he carried me away.

"Safety override code your grandfather had installed. He paid for the 'hances so he installed a code to keep them from firing on him. He gave it to me and your father."

"Did I make the right decision?" I asked.

We turned the bend of the sewer and Pumpernickel turned to face the direction we were headed and picked up his pace. "I don't know Ms. Pascuzzo. But I hope we did."

With a tower's worth of processors, I still ponder the question. Even with every processor in the Valley at my disposal, I still doubt I'd settle on a comfortable answer.

***

I sat in a metal chair. The burn on my shoulder was bandaged with white gauze. Three hundred and fifty-seven probes were attached to my scalp. My hair was a mess from the events in the sewers and the neurogel that helped seal the connection between the probes and my mind. I was not tied into the chair, but there were slack straps in case it became necessary

I was far from the sewers, the room smelled like antiseptic. Far from my family, three hovercar rides away. The basement of an unknown building was far from the Crest Tower Penthouse of my grandfather.

The only sound I'd made since Pumpernickel dropped me off with the Baumein scientists was a startled squeal when they led me into this basement room and set my eyes on what was waiting for me.

I still had a hard time facing the monstrosity in front of me.

I still have a hard time facing myself.

But the one glance I took was more than enough to remember every detail about what sat in front of me that night. What I am today.

Across the room, a three-meter tall vat was filled with bubbling blue liquid. My head floated in it so large I could see the pores around my nose without needing a vanity mirror. Its eyes were closed peacefully. Its mouth was at a neutral rest. Its brow was unwrinkled. Not a single thought moved through its head.

Using my genetic sample that was on file with Baumein they cloned my head. If they could get away with only cloning my brain I'm sure they would've. It grew over the course of weeks when the test results were first validated. The scientists were informed before the teachers and students, likely to avoid fiascos like the one my grandfather had orchestrated in the sewers.

They enlarged the whole thing to give the clone more neural pathways than any brain needed. Put the head in a nutrient bath and waited for me to be delivered so they could transfer my mind to the new head.

The head in the vat was bald. Whatever gene made hair was eliminated. My cheeks and upper lip were void of small hairs. Countless teen girls would kill for that, all I saw was a face uncannily like my own. My head didn't have any eyebrows either. Scientists deemed them superfluous for the job I'd be employed to do.

Instead of hair floating off my head and into the bubbling stream of the vat countless wires were embedded in my skin and through my skull. They floated out of the vat and wired into the ceiling. They would soon, connect me to the tower I was in.

A scientist lowered a blue holoscreen in front of my face. A puzzle showed up on it. I solved it easily. Another appeared and I solved it. They were similar to the ASLAN, a few were more difficult, took more thinking, and made me come at the problem in a unique direction.

Despite the challenges I always solved the puzzle. When I needed to see it from a new direction I always seemed to be able to flex my mind that way.

After the 128th puzzle was solved the scientist announced that the transfer was complete. They didn't direct the comment at me, the scientists talked to me as little as they could get away with.

Without a puzzle in front of me, I didn't know what to do next.

I looked up. My vision was still tinted blue as if a holoscreen couldn't be lifted away from my face. Silver bubbles over my vision as I watched the scientists lift my small body out of the chair and onto a gurney. She looked peaceful. Eyes closed, mouth neutral, brow relaxed not a thought in her head. They wheeled the body out of the basement flipping the lights off on the way out.

I was a towermind.

Requests for transaction approval, calculations, and elevator scheduling arrived for me to handle. There were more puzzles to solve.

I would take care of them in due time.

The first command I executed was turning the lights back on in my basement room.

The Hacked Manticore

The spider cut through the face of the corrugated metal crate. The six legs of the woman were able to cling to the face of the crate. Her arms were 'hanced with cutting torches, welders, and a dozen other metalwork tools. Sparks flew away from the cut and towards the crowd of forklifts.

A heavy-duty hovertruck had dropped off the crate less than a minute ago. Dozens of dockworkers hovered near the new prize. Their vehicles formed a flat wall, each one's microfuser calculating exactly how close they could get without getting squished by the face of the crate when it fell open. Every driver needed this shipment, it could be the last one this shift. Herbert knew there wasn't enough inside for all of them.

The vehicles once sported a uniform orange paint job, back when only AIs navigated them. But when humans took back control of the docks they graffitied the equipment with neon spray paint and covered the bumpers and roofs with art and obscenities, not that there was a big difference in the eyes of a dockworker. The swarm, waiting restlessly, looked like a high Valley billboard advertising colorful static because a hacker got into the feed.

Despite the diverse paint jobs each vehicle that hovered in the air had the same double-pronged magnetic tusk design, similar to old-style forklifts. A proprietary design that made it impossible to interface with shipments without using the Baumein conglomerate's tech.

Tech that was updated regularly to allegedly limit smuggling contraband into the Valley. But all it did, in Herbert's eyes, was keep dock workers like him from owning equipment. Anything he bought would be outdated in a fiscal quarter. Deep Valley mobsters seemed to always innovate ways to smuggle. Drivers seemed to never innovate ways to update their tech.

The tusks were the only similarity to the archaic forklifts. Modern forklifts floated in the air since navigation through 3D space was necessary to efficiently move the Valley's supplies. These lifts also had enough CPUs jammed into them to process the cyberton of navigational data required for efficient deliveries.

The lift's cockpit was cozy. Hardly big enough to fit a human torso. But that's all Herbert needed.

Herbert's microfuser burnt hot on the left side of his face. The silver towers of microchips inserted into the skin and bones around his left eye and back towards his cerebellum were tiny computers that only scratched the surface of his driving interface.

A chrome flatworm cable ran from his left cheek to the dashboard of his lift. But just a flatworm would give him the imprecise control of an executive's chauffeur. Cylindrical metal ports ran down his spine linking him with thick wires to the back of his vehicle's cockpit. He was tied in as tightly as a snail in a shell. The neuro-bandwidth given by the ports enabled him to operate the vehicle at high speeds. The kinds of speeds necessary to stay on top of the chart, employed, and maybe eating a hot meal.

His legs were dead weight. He'd had them replaced with bionic ones years ago so that he could fit in the lift. His bionic replacements were sitting in the bay he'd rented today's lift from, waiting for him to finish his shift. Right now the nerves for his legs controlled the vehicle with neural connectors that provided more precision than a gas pedal, brake, and clutch ever could.

Shirtless, shirts held in heat and heat lead to overclocking, Herbert smelled the salty bay breeze that flowed through his cockpit. No real lift had a windshield or doors. His goggles blocked the wind from his eyes, everything else needed the coolant.

He hunched over the dashboard, 'hanced eyes watching the spider's progress, waiting for her to finish the third and final cut. His forearms were attached to the dash through neural connectors. The nerves of his amputated hands interfaced directly with the machine.

The entire vehicle was an extension of his body. He was a manticore, like every other worker on the docks. A human meshed with true machines, not just machines imitating or improving on biology. Every day manticores like him flew through the docks, fighting for rank and a hearty commission.

Just like in the Valley, high-altitude positions were coveted. From a high spot, you could snag a box as soon as the crate's wall fell. Above Herbert, manticores jockeyed for higher positions. He was mid-pack, focusing on doing the work efficiently rather than using tactics like altitude.

The spider finished her cut, and scurried along to the next crate, a swarm had already formed in front of it. The loose corrugated sheet of metal fell centimeters from Herbert's pronged tusks, just as he'd calculated.

Herbert rushed forward to claim a package to increase his total shipments for the day. He snatched one on his tusk and buzzed out of the way, as more manticores flew in to grab their share.

Herbert navigated his forklift through the narrow gaps in traffic. His box was just this side of the lift's capacity, shippers always keep the boxes as packed as possible. The crate's data streamed in through the lift's tusks. His spinal implants communicated predictive courses of other vehicles to his legs and arms for steering. His microfuser filled out paperwork registering the shipment. His flesh brain was the maestro of them all.

In the early days of the docks, AIs did the work fast. Manticores were built to do it faster. Conglomerate execs were agnostic about who did the work, as long as the margins were fat.

Machine enhancements enabled dockworkers to exterminate AI lifts. High performance was what maintained their extinction. If record numbers of crates didn't get moved every shift, AIs would be uploaded from the hard drives they hibernated in.

His 'hanced right eye spotted a buzzing lift take a minor detour from the predicted path. He caught it milliseconds before his spine notified him.

The nerves wired into his vehicle reacted on gut instinct, not binary calculations. Herbert dodged the ensuing chaos. Some lifts were too late. The vehicles crashed, and the contents of the boxes littered to the ground of the dock. His electronic eardrums automatically muted the deafening explosion.

Three-dimensional collisions were always a mess. The floor of the dock was littered with piles of scrap. Metal, flesh, bones, and silicon. Deep Valley kids or Saints could comb through it. To the conglomerates, it was a write-off and cost of doing business.

Anything could have caused the driver to detour. But the most common cause, in Herbert's experience, was manticores overclocking themselves trying to get as many shipments on their account before end of shift. Everything was a balance on the dock, from the crates to their operators. Galleria Valley had equipment that needed to move and the manticores were key.

Herbert slowed down just enough to drop the cargo off on the elevator that would carry it to the correct level of Galleria Valley. As soon as the magnetic tusks confirmed it was free he shifted the lift into a low gear to accelerate himself into the fast lane of traffic hoping to find a fresh crate.

Tavid messaged him while scanning the dock for a spider.

"Crash 152 sorrow it, ya?" Tavid felt worried about the driver. The text data was clipped but laced with emotion from the neural connectors. It was impossible to send a coherent message in this hyper-aware state. It was also impossible not to send your raw self across the lines.

"Caught me not," Herbert replied. Frustration he was trying to ignore seeped into the message. He sped up his microfuser to handle the conversation. His temple burned but not uncomfortably. It was what the warmth he always wanted in the drafty low tower apartments he lived in as a kid.

"Safety true."

"Dead no spend no cred." The words were a bastardization of their childhood saying, but it was sent with all the fascination of watching dock explosion as kids and dreaming of what it'd be like to trade your limbs for a chance at a paycheck.

There were no spiders to chase to crates. Spiders always clocked out early, leaving crates sealed for the next shift. Herbert'd done well today, currently ranked low forties, but he needed more to hold the position.

The shift bell rang through the dock notifying Herbert of what he already knew to be true.

Nearly every single lift in the dock turned to race back to the bay where the rental lifts were returned. Lifts were used right to end of shift, but every second past the bell cared a late fee. The lucky few who owned their forklifts carried a couple remaining boxes to the elevators. This would scrape up a few more points for them. And change the leaderboard stats out of Herbert's favor.

***

Herbert parked the lift inside the small two-meter cube bay. Despite the size it was easy to land thanks to Herbert's hyperawareness of the vehicle's maneuverability. He placed it down easily inside the graffitied metal walls of the bay.

His navy blue metallic legs approached, two chrome hands rested where his torso would soon sit. There were no toes on the feet and the knees were just large hinges that lacked the side-to-side movement of a flesh knee. It was a compromise he was willing to make since he wasn't some 'hanced bouncer who needed to compete with the unenhanced.

He was a manticore. He performed in the docks against other manticores, at speeds that would leave even the fastest legs in the dust. And as the metal ports on his back detached from the lift he could already feel that speed fading.

He pulled the nubs of his forearms out of the lift's dash.

From the ceiling of the bay spindly arms folded out. They were there to do automatic maintenance and repairs on the lift. But first, they did their best to place Herbert's hands onto his arms. There was always a little adjusting to get the hands to respond correctly.

The hands were an economic model just like the legs and just as easy to maintain and repair. But they were still an improvement over his first. A set of three-fingered hands. He bought these nice ones the first time he ranked above 25 on the leader board, ages ago.

With five digits and three joints each he could shave with a razor and pull his long hair into a ponytail. However, the fingers lacked the sensory feedback to feel any individual hair on his head.

Once he was happy enough with how his hands were seated and integrated with his nerves the bay's arms lifted him onto his legs.

Again, it took a few adjustments to get the neural connection right. After a few tries of reseating himself, he settled with the fact no legs would ever be as maneuverable as the lift.

Herbert was running at microfuser rates, faster than his natural flesh mind, but still lagging behind lift speeds. The small computer implanted around his eye wasn't nearly as powerful as the lift.

The microfuser speeds helped him get the sensation of walking back under him. Each step was analyzed by the computer giving him feedback on his form. He felt like a drunk toddler as he moved toward the locker that held his few belongings.

He pulled on his loose-fitting shirt, the fabric was thin and left room for the ports on his back. He shrugged his forest green rain jacket over his shoulders. His metal fingers always had trouble threading the tiny zipper due to their limited sensors. But it'd be raining in the Valley, it was always raining in the Valley, and he wanted to take care of the chore now.

Once he was zipped to the chin he pulled his gym bag out of the room's locker and slung it over his shoulder. It held his toiletries, his one change of clothes, and a few nicknacks. It bounced against his metal hip as he walked out of the lift bay. The motion would've irritated him... if he could feel it.

Walking through the concrete corridors that lead to the Valley Herbert slowed his microprocessor down completely. Once he was at flesh speeds time felt like it sped past him since it took so long to think through and complete actions.

He reviewed the dock's leaderboard through a popup window the microfuser displayed over his vision. Just reading his name and rank felt like a slow waltz.

Herbert found he'd landed in the top one hundred. Too many owner-drivers around today and they knocked him out of the top 50.

Tavid did worse finishing second from last. Eleventh from last if you counted the nine drivers who'd wrecked throughout the shift. But nobody counted them.

You got good pay if you landed in the top fifty. Hundred or more and the payout was just enough to cover the rent on the lift and the day's license fee. Only owner-operated manticores landed in the top ten, which was where the real money was.

The damned owner-operators could afford cutting-edge bionics, faster lifts, and the ability to carry heavier crates because of it. Plus they had the standing to get smuggled goods into the elevators. Thus funding higher-end bionics. A virtuous cycle once you are there. As long as you could stay at the top.

Too many days out of the top ten and debt piled up. Herbert would have the same problem if he was out of the top 100 for too long. But for an owner-operator missed mob shipments could lead to disappearances. Payments on the owned lift piled up since it was technically not owned but mortgaged with high-interest rates. Elders forbid if they repoed your bionics, that'd make you late for a shift, assuming you could get off of whatever stool they placed you on.

For all those reasons it was best to push yourself as hard as you could. Overclock and crash to the bottom of the dock. At least then you died a manticore. Herbert had never been sure which was worse. Living at the bottom of the charts or the top.

However, unlike the buildings in the Valley, there was always a space at the top of the leaderboard. That's part of what made being a manticore so freeing. The charts welcomed anyone quick enough to grab a high position. Many considered it better to live like an executive for a fiscal quarter than a long life eating slop out of algae vats and crawling into sleeping pods every night.

Herbert downloaded the credits he'd earned for the day minus the expenses for the lift. Ninety percent of the remaining pay covered the debt he owed on the bionic legs and hands. Ten percent was left for him and it'd buy him a bowl of noodles. It might pay for a pod for the night if the noodles were cold.

Heading down the corridors that led to Galleria Valley's food court he used his microfuser to call Tavid and figure out his friend's plan for dinner.

"I'm cleaning up wreckage with the Saints next shift," Tavid said. "We could use your help. Free vat chili in it for you."

The slow-spoken sentences full of words to convey all his meaning weren't laced with emotion like they had been in the docks. But they still had Tavid's heart in them. He always counted the few that fell off the leaderboard and to the bottom of the docks.

"And get my head torn off the cross traffic?" Herbert scoffed. "Just to recover some overclock's remnant."

"That could've been us."

"Not if we're careful. I'm going to the food court to catch the game. It's safer."

"Not by much. Keep your head down."

"You too. I'm only there to watch a game and eat something other than algae. Stay safe yeah?"

"The dead don't spend no cred," Tavid replied then disconnected.

Herbert walked out of the dock's corridors and into the rainy neon city of Galleria Valley. Skyscrapers and billboards loomed over him. Puddles of water collected in the street, drains clogged or non-existent. His toeless metal feet sloshed through them, unable to feel the icy chill of the water.

A cold wind blew through the canyon-like streets. The hair on the nape of his neck stood up and he could each of them. The ports on his back caught the cold too. The skin near them flexed and constricted around them in response. He pulled the hood of his rain jacket over his head. Doing his best to protect the little flesh he had left.

***

The Valley's food court was filled with uneven rows of makeshift food stands. The vendors here were unpredictable like overclocked manticores on the dock, except here the vendors thankfully stayed behind their counters. Shop stalls were delineated by walls of broken concrete and scrap rebar. The stalls were filled with makeshift kitchen equipment and fierce chefs. The cooks had to be fierce to hold down their stall. If they were lucky, they'd cook in one place until their ingredients ran out, but sometimes threats of competing vendors pushed them out before their ingredients were used up.

The court was a maze, instead of neat hallways like the corridors of the dock. A patron could easily find themselves at a dead end, a greedy vendor shouting about the quality of the food he was selling and vague threats about what would happen if you ate with his competitors.

It wasn't a friendly place, but that wasn't a shock for somewhere this deep in the Valley. Herbert settled with the lousy company. He couldn't afford anything prepared by an auto-chef and didn't want the Saint's vat chili for the fourth night in a row. The best he could do was navigate the maze towards the center hoping to get noodles made with more wheat than sawdust.

The entire plaza had once been Lieberman's Caliber Tower, a hulking skyscraper that housed entire manufacturing industries. It held the Lieberman conglomerate's headquarters and most of their execs lived there for the convenient elevator commute. During the War of Acquisition, the tower fell, literally. In an instant it became rubble. Thousands of rooms and bodies crumbled to the floor of the Valley.

Herbert only ever knew the plaza as a food court, but old manticores told stories about the war and net videos still played the scraper's destruction. All active conglomerates claimed the attack, which was a sure sign none of them were responsible. Why, how, and who did it was never uncovered. And the diaspora of Lieberman execs couldn't hold the conglomerate together after the building's demolition.

Denizens of the Valley, who never could've afforded to live in the scraper itself, immediately rummaged through the scrap. They made the best of what they found. Weapons went to the gangs, scrap concrete and metals built up walls and roofs to shelter them from the rain, bodies went to the sewers or the stews.

Rats found homes in the ruins, and so did grass and edible plants. The occupants found they had something of value they could sell. The war kept conglomerates busy and taxes low.

By the time the war ended the bottom of the Valley had its claws so deep into the ruins that it'd take another war to dig the folks out. Herbert figured by now there was enough mob money in here to keep the conglomerates out regardless of how hard they fought. But the execs would never admit it.

The remaining two conglomerates, Baumein and Mandlestadt, divvied up the corporations they'd acquired, splitting the towers of the Valley up as evenly as crooked lawyers could. Both sides laid claim to the destruction of Caliber Tower, so both claimed the ruins. Which all but guaranteed that no one but deep Valley citizens would ever use this plaza again.

Herbert always felt like contesting the land was a bit of a cop-out by the execs. The company could claim it as a loss on their balance sheets, and since it was a contested zone they could claim it was their competitor's job to fix it up. The vendors and mobs didn't seem to mind the disregard. And Herbert appreciated having somewhere to eat a cheap meal.

Near the center of the maze, Herbert found a noodle shop. Behind the scrap wood counter, steaming pots of milky broth spread nutty aromas into the air. The hot noodles carried a high price, especially on a cold evening like this. He figured he could sleep soundly on one of the Saint's bunks if his belly was full of a warm meal.

Rain pattered on the plastic awning that hung above him. Cold wind blew droplets off the edges and into the noodle shop.

The cook placed a chipped ceramic bowl in front of Herbert. Steam danced up into his nose a savory meaty flavor, even if he couldn't afford extra for the meat itself. A lump of noodles peaked out of the murky white broth like an island in the sea. Herbert didn't want to know what kind of bones were broken down to make the soup. He just knew it would taste better than algae.

The cook didn't stop shouting about the meal, having a customer in front of the shop seemed to increase his vigor. His electronic vocal cords carried his voice like a PA system. Unfortunately, every other vendor in the court had the same implant leading to a cacophony of menu items.

Herbert muted the sounds with his electronic eardrums, using his microfuser to set up a filter specifically for the vendors' speaking frequency. Nice thing about inorganic voices was they were easy to filter.

He ate his hot noodles in peace tuning into a free sonicball game on his microfuser. It wasn't the latest game played in the league but the reruns were free and Herbert was far enough behind on the sport that he didn't mind.

When there were only a few slurps of noodles two people joined him at the bar, sitting on both sides of him. He didn't like it. Especially when they didn't order.

"Are you Herbert F. Lang?" The man on his left asked.

Herbert looked up. The thin guy wore a black suit, white undershirt, and neatly knotted tie. His hair matched the suit in color and was cut evenly like a bowl was placed upside down on his head. It was surely one of the approved conglomerate haircuts. The microfuser embedded around his left eye flashed with RGB lights.

"Who's asking?" Herbert replied skeptical of anyone wearing a suit this deep in the Valley.

"We've got a job for you, manti," the second one said from behind him. He turned and saw a woman who barely fit into a matching suit.

Every cubic centimeter of the suit's shoulders and chest was filled. The silver chrome hands poking out of the cuffs explained why. Chrome reached up around her neck but stopped at her sharp jawline. Everything from the neck up was organic except for the microfuser around her eye. From the quality of the hands alone Herbert knew she had high tech 'hances under the suit.

Company policy was to stuff it all away in a suit. A gang member would've worn as little as possible to make sure everyone knew what they were packing. She likely picked a suit one size too small to toe the line between the two sides.

"Respectfully, I already have one." Of course, she was aware of this. Otherwise, she wouldn't have called him a manti.

"I'm Associate Yamamoto and this is Associate Gomez. We're here to offer a job more important than delivering executive-grade underwear," the man said.

"I prefer not to get involved with conglomerate affairs." Herbert loudly slurped the last of his noodles and set the bowl down gently on the counter.

He had more sense than to get involved with businessmen like this. Only conglomerate bureaucracy could be coldly indifferent to you. Gang members, at least, cared where they dumped your body so they could avoid getting caught. If he'd ranked lower today he might've been open to their smuggling job, but tonight he had enough money to get by.

"Someone spent a lot of money on me to make me difficult to turn down." The woman extended her fingers, then closed them into a fist in front of Herbert's face to make sure he'd noticed them.

He recognized the model as something he could never dream of affording.

"I assure you it was money well spent. It'd be easier for me to turn down a beautiful companion for the evening than you." He stepped away from the bar.

"Except a companion isn't going to pay you," she replied from close behind him, easily matching his stride.

The man quickly caught up to them huffing. Herbert suspected there were slow flesh legs under his pants.

"What do 'glom lackeys like you need to smuggle something for?"

"Never said it was a smuggling job," the man answered between heavy breaths.

Herbert stopped walking. No one hired a manticore to do more than move crates. There were bigger brawn and brains for those jobs. "What kind of job is it then?"

Herbert's feet were resting in a puddle he didn't care. Both the suits avoided it to protect the mirror polish of their shoes.

"You interested?" the woman asked.

"I'm interested in getting to bed. What's a manticore good for other than delivery?"

The businessman looked up at the sky, the weather had turned from a dreary rain to a light drizzle. He pulled a pack of cigarettes out of his inner coat pocket.

"Baumein's got a new vehicle." He offered a cigarette to Herbert. "We need someone used to moving quick to drive it."

Herbert accepted the cigarette. He shoved the gift into his pocket. Might be able to trade it for a better bunk at the Saints.

"An elevator won't do?" Herbert asked. Standard hovercar drivers weren't perfect, but they were on corporate payroll.

"Tried that. They're too slow." The woman answered without looking at him. Unsurprisingly the suits were starting to gain unwanted attention in the food court. "So we're moving on to giving you manties a shot."

"There are a few thousand manticores at the dock? Why me?" Herbert asked.

The man dragged on his cigarette the tip sizzled in the wet air. He exhaled out the side of his mouth, caring more about the present company than those walking past him.

"You consistently rank top 100 on the dock's leaderboards," he said, "and you're clean of gang involvement as far as we care to tell.

There are about ten drivers like you that fit the bill. You're at the top of the list."

The businessman pinched the cigarette between his lips and pulled a glass tablet out of his jacket pocket. Herbert always wondered how many pockets were in those suit jackets. The man placed the tablet in Herbert's hand and the glass clinked against his metal palm.

"Review this and show up to the Anodyze Building at start of shift tomorrow. We've got to find a couple more drivers tonight."

The man dropped his cigarette butt into the puddle at Herbert's feet. It hissed like a blown fuse. He walked away headed to the edge of the food court as fast as his flesh legs could carry him.

Herbert looked up at the woman. "You said Baumein's got a new car. But Anodyze is owned by Mandlestadt."

The woman smiled with soft pink lips and shrugged. The gesture pushed her suit's seams to their limits. Herbert heard at least one of them snap, thanks to his electric ear drums.

In three quick strides, she was at the man's side deterring the few denizens of the shadow from approaching him.

Herbert didn't trust his slick metal fingers to hold onto the glass tablet. He slipped it into his jacket pocket next to the cigarette. He fumbled with the pocket's zipper, his fingers not deft enough for the tab. After a moment he sealed the trinkets inside, safe from the rain and prying hands.

He'd finally made it to the top of a list. That was a dream he'd pursued since childhood.

But he wasn't sure this was the right list to be on.

***

The padding that dug into Herbert's armpit chafed him. The padding rubbing against the tip of his nose irritated him. The padding under his waist, where his legs should be, scratched him. And the guy holding the briefcase Herbert was stored in swung the case with every step.

The inside of the briefcase was pitch black. His 'hanced eyes had a low light mode, but that required there to be some light. The only thing that lit up in this case was his microfuser and it merely illuminated the black closed cell padding in front of him.

The briefcase jostled and Herbert's head hit the foam in front of him. It didn't hurt anything more than his pride. If the pay was anything less than life changing he'd resent the situation.

But the payout for finishing the job and coming back with a Baumein car could put him at the top of the charts for at least half a year. It'd pay off the debt on his limbs, maybe enable him to put a good down payment on new ones. Or increase his cerebral 'hances.

Presently Herbert had no limbs attached. That's how he fit snuggly into the briefcase.

He went into the case willingly. He'd signed a contract agreeing to do it, along with a dozen other tasks, before his shift started.

The contract had to be signed to get the check. The risks had to be accepted and Mandlestadt's responsibility had to be waived. The four other manticores did it without a second thought. Herbert refused to be left behind.

After a full body scan of his torso for the briefcase padding the Mandlestadt scientists began their test.

The first few were fine. The corporate doctor, in her long white lab coat with an embroidered Mandlestadt logo on the chest pocket, assured him it was a standard medical physical.

Herbert took the doctor at her word since he'd never seen a doctor for something so mundane. Only doctors he visited were deep in the

Valley. And those visits focused on loping off flesh limbs and arranging nerves for neural efficient connections. An expensive procedure, but a price every manticore paid for the chance to work on the dock.

After the physical, the doctor wheeled him through Anodyze Tower's hallways and down the elevators. Herbert was not approved to use his legs inside the tower for "security concerns." So the doctor pushed him on a short gurney, seemingly made for manticores.

He arrived in a testing room with the other five other manticores. They had the same setup as him. A doctor pushing a gurney. Leaned back but not quite comfortable.

Despite the building's frigid air conditioning, they all lay shirtless. Shirts insulated heat and overheating led to overclocking.

One by one the five manticores were lifted off their gurney and placed on a circular neural connector. The connector was the same type Herbert used to connect to his legs, except this one was mounted on top of a metal box.

The doctors transferred each manticore with indifference. As if they were simply plugging a power cable into the wall.

Herbert was placed on the neural connector and immediately realized he was a dozen centimeters shorter than normal. He would've stood eye level with the docs on his bionic legs, instead, he had to look up to them like a child.

A box with neural connectors for his arms sat in before him. It was a trapezoidal design with a screen on the back for the doctors to monitor. Anything Herbert needed to know would be transmitted through his microfuser.

Herbert inserted his residual limbs into the circular neural connectors. He adjusted them until the connection was comfortable. Which was more than he could do with his waist.

Mandlestadt was known for its efficiency. So it wasn't shocking that he was centimeters from the woman who was placed down before him on his left.

The woman was lean with small shoulders and thin arms. Long amber hair poked out from her armpits. It matched her short hair that swept back on her scalp like she was driving a lift at full speed despite being stationary. Her bare breasts were small and covered in scars the size and shape of rice grains. Matching scars covered her stomach but didn't reach to her back. They were likely burn marks from working as a spider in the docks.

Hot hands of the spiders threw sparks every which way when cutting into new shipments. Protective padding would insulate and overheat. It was cheaper to get a cerebral enhancement to increase your pain tolerance than to risk overclocking.

She was already leaning forward distracted by something on her microfuser, as disinterested as the doctors in the world around her.

The last manticore was a scruffy talkative man. His hair was long and shaggy but not long enough to pull into a ponytail like Herbert's. His chest was covered with curly black hairs and his face hadn't been shaved in a week.

He made jokes at the doctors about how they were carrying him, the doctors didn't acknowledge his comments let alone laugh. The scruffy-looking man was the last to be plugged in located to Herbert's right. The man was so close to Herbert that he could smell the old algae stew on his breath.

Herbert didn't want to think about the man. But sitting in the dark in a swinging briefcase there was nothing else to think about.

Wires came down from the ceiling and plugged into the manticore's spinal ports. The feeling was familiar if not a little cold. Typically lifts were still warm from their last driver. These connectors hadn't been used in at least a shift, likely longer.

The tests were simple at first. Solve puzzles to get used to the integration with the neural connectors. His microfuser showed a screen over his vision that aided his interaction with the puzzle.

His back was plugged into a high-powered computer, more powerful than anything that would fit in a lift. It took a moment to get the computer meshed with his mind, these tests gauged helped him integrate. Herbert took control of the extra CPUs without a problem. Any manticore worth their algae could do it.

A cool breeze blew through the room. It wasn't a muggy salty wind like the docks. It was crisp and dry. It smelled of antiseptic. It made Herbert's back shiver which rattled the cords that connected him to the roof. The cool air was necessary to keep them from overheating. Overheating led to overclocking.

But other things led to overclocking as well.

The puzzles turned into 3D mazes. Those mazes turned into navigating a city. Herbert's microfuser played a driving simulator over his vision. It wasn't as immersive as a VR game, but the challenges were certainly more advanced.

He wouldn't be shocked if they had him playing against the building's AI. Some brain hidden away in the basement under sub-zero conditions, wired into all of Anodyze Tower's equipment.

Herbert rounded a corner at high speed while solving a navigational equation for the next turn when the game cut out for the first time.

He felt like he'd splatted into the building. The docs looked towards the end of the row, the woman on Herbert's left blocked his view. No one explained anything and the game resumed shortly.

Herbert ran at hyper-aware speeds his mind moving so fast that an hour felt like a week. The scientists observing him moved in slow motion behind the popup of his microfuser. His heartbeat plodded along against his chest despite being elevated according to his microfuser.

He dodged in and out of buildings in the test. The puzzle began to drop buildings around him to increase the difficulty. It was no different than avoiding crashes on the docks.

Herbert's world began to feel fuzzy as he thought through the solution to two navigational problems at once, needing both of them prepared in case the computer threw a building at him. The edges of the buildings began to blur, along with the scientists behind him.

Sweat rolled down his brow and back, weaving its way around his nose and through the ports on his spine. He missed the ice-cold breeze from earlier. His microfuser reported the external temp had only decreased since the start of the experiment. He wondered which was broken, his biology or the computer.

The navigation of the city and its obstacles had pushed him to spin up parts of his mind he hadn't in years. Parts of his mind opened up that he'd locked off years ago. The computers wired into his back gave his mind space to grow. Neurons fired that'd been dormant for years.

Herbert watched Tavid as a young boy ran through the lab a bundle of scrap in his scrawny arms. Saw his father throw a bottle across the room, not out of anger, but out of a misfiring neural connector on his bionic arm.

A building appeared in front of him in the game. He fired off the navigational equation he'd just solved. He skidded past the obstacle, losing some points for the poor navigation. He had to corral his mind back under control. Had to use these old parts of his mind for work, not memories. Otherwise, it'd run away from him like a rat hiding in dock scraps.

He saw rats scurry between the scientists' feet and climb down the wires from the ceiling. Watched them crawl over the amber-haired woman's shoulders down her arms. He felt them crawling on his back weaving between his spinal ports. There was no way rats would be allowed in a pristine Mandlestadt building.

He'd never run this fast on the docks. Wouldn't dare. There was no rank on the leaderboard worth it. But the Mandlestadt paycheck was more than any day in the dock could promise him.

He saw his name at the top of a leaderboard, he erased the names and numbers. He needs the space to solve a new navigational equation. He calculated new trajectories for his simulated ship double checking them to keep his mind busy.

Something whizzed past his ear. He thought it was another rogue memory. His microfuser reported that his electronic eardrums had contributed to the simulated sound. The game had added an enemy ship and that ship was firing at Herbert from behind. Yet another obstacle to navigate.

Herbert was doing the work of three manticores, maybe more. At these speeds, he could have an argument with himself and firmly believe both sides. He could tell himself original jokes and laugh at the surprising punchline.

Herbert's simulation cut out. His high-speed processing did not.

The man next to him groaned.

Herbert turned his head to look. The movement was quick, but he observed it in slow motion. The disconnect made him woozy.

The scruffy man's eyes were crossed looking at the tip of his nose. His pupils dilated then constricted, the muscles seemed not to know what to focus on.

The man's body shivered. The only reason he didn't fall off the table was the neural connectors and wires hooked into his back. The wires rattled with his quick movement like machine gun fire.

The room's cool breeze wafted the man's breath into Herbert's face. It smelled like an old dinner, old algae stew but was now mixed with copper and tin. Herbert could pick each note out with his mind like they were crates in a new shipment.

The scruffy man's jaw went limp. Inside his open mouth, the tongue flopped against teeth and pallets. Herbert's electronic eardrums picked up every wet slap of the tongue.

Saliva foamed up around the scruffy man's lips. It dribbled down onto his bare chest interlocking with the curly hairs. Then it dripped onto the Mandlestadt equipment.

The man's torso went limp.

Bent at the elbows the man leaned forward. His chest fell short of resting on the trapezoidal platform where his arms were connected. The tension of the wires in his back held him up but dangling.

Herbert stared at the man for what felt like an hour but his micro-fuser reported was merely seconds. Herbert was so focused he could count the hairs on the man's chest and even group them by which curled clockwise and which curled counterclockwise if he wanted.

All Herbert wanted to do was look away.

The test resumed, and a semitransparent screen blocked Herbert's view of the scruffy manticore. A new building immediately popped into Herbert's flight path. He calculated a divergent course glad to have something to focus on other than the man.

In Herbert's peripheral vision, he saw the scientists clean the man's saliva off the equipment in slow motion. It looked like they were moving slowly to be delicate with the drool. But that was a distortion of Herbert's hyper-awareness. In reality, they were using a disposable rag.

Herbert focused all of his mind on the game. Avoiding any more thoughts of the overclocked man.

Until now.

Sitting in the dark of the briefcase the scruffy manticore was the only thing that seemed to come up in Herbert's mind. This dark briefcase didn't unlock his mind like high-speed computers. But it didn't provide Herbert with any distractions. Despite running at flesh speed the details of the incident were crystal clear.

He wondered what kind of beast this Baumein car was. Too much for an elevator to handle. So much so that Mandlestadt scientists designed tests that overclocked two manticore candidates.

The paycheck was worth it. It'd pay off Herbert's debts, maybe Tavid's too. It'd get him a lift of his own so he could work extra on a shift and rank top 10 on the leaderboard. Something his younger self couldn't dream of.

Herbert had passed the tests. No one told him his rank. He didn't care. He knew he was in the top three, and that was good enough.

The scientists removed the manticore torsos, down the line in the same order they'd inserted them, placing the manticores on a short gurney or in a small body bag depending on their heartbeat.

Muffled talking came from outside the briefcase. Herbert adjusted his electronic eardrum to try to understand the conversation. The padding was too thick for him to make out any specifics.

Then he heard popping.

It sounded like someone was lightly thumping on thick steel. The thumping repeated so quickly that it was impossible to believe that anything but a machine could be that fast.

The sound stopped.

The latch of Herbert's briefcase clicked. His handler opened the front panel. Bright florescent light caused Herberts 'hanced eyes to blind him with white. The white receded to black as the electronic irises tightened and overcorrected.

Before his vision could normalize he was being lifted from under his bare arms. The associate that moved him had cold metallic hands that made his skin tingle.

Herbert was placed on the soft gel of a neural connector. The needles of the neural connector injected into his waist. It prickled but it was better than the scratchy padding of the briefcase. The handler must have placed him in the car.

Once his eyes settled on the right exposure Herbert didn't know what to think.

He sat in an expansive room with colorful sheet metal paintings hung on the wall. Hallways led out of the room, two were blocked with heavy blast shields. To Herbert's left the third hallway had a few Mandlestadt associates with rifles near it. A pile of scrap metal that was once security bots sat under the arch of the doorway.

The neural connector under him was on a metal box similar to the testing room. A pair of neural connectors for his forearms sat in front of him. Instead of being a harsh trapezoidal shape, it was a smooth silver dome.

There were three docks placed in a triangle shape so a manticore set in each one could see the other two. There was no obsession with efficient placement. Someone could walk between the manticores without an issue.

All three docks had smooth chamfered edges and intricate decorative carvings. The wires that hung from the ceiling were tied in neat bundles only branching out at the bottom where they needed to connect to spinal ports.

The focus on aesthetics was a clear sign they were in a Baumein building. No Mandlestadt accountant would approve such lavish designs.

To his left, the amber-haired woman Herbert tested next to was already placed in position and hunched over with forearms inserted into the dome. On his right Associate Gomez, the heavily 'hanced woman who'd offered Herbert this job, placed the third manticore on the dock.

He'd yet to meet the third manticore. She had long blonde hair that draped over her right shoulder. The left side of her head was shaved to the skin exposing the metal streaks of her imbedded microfuser. A starburst tattoo seemed to extend the streak of the microfuser to the base of her skull and neck.

Her skin was smooth aside from the scars around her waist and forearms that every manticore had. Her breasts took up most of her chest and they hung away from her body as she leaned over to insert her arms into the controls. She wasn't as lean as the other manticore. She had a small belly that sat right above the neural connector.

She bristled and arched her broad shoulders as the wires connected to her back. Herbert did the same as his connection. The ports were cold and smelled of flowers. He wasn't expecting such a rare artificial scent.

Loud repetitive gunshots fired from his left. All three manticores looked, although the amber-haired one had a difficult time seeing anything since it happened behind her. Herbert watched it without a problem.

Three Mandlestadt associates with snug-fitting suits and compact machine guns pulled tight against their chests fired down a hallway.

Human voices shouted down the hallway. Baumein hadn't waited long to get their 'hanced security detail on the job.

"Let's get this show on the road," Associate Gomez said once it appeared the blonde manticore was situated.

"Where's the car we're supposed to steal?" Herbert asked. The words came out quickly as his thought processes sped up as he integrated with the machine.

Gomez picked up her rifle which was leaning against the briefcase her manticore came out of. "Never said it was a car. This whole tower's a vehicle and we need to get it across the Valley to the Anodyze building."

Herbert poured through the data he was linked into. Gomez was correct, there were hover lift thrusters built into the tower designed to carry the top twelve floors away. It wasn't clear what was inside the building. That information was encrypted and Herbert didn't have the keys to get in.

What he did have access to was a multitude of sensors around the exterior of the building. He could see hovercars of security detail circling the building. Microphones picked up the scoff of wind buffeting his sides. The sides of the building.

Forklifts were an extension of the manticore's body on the dock. He felt like a buzzing hornet when he drove them. This twelve-floor monstrosity that came to a point like a pyramid made him feel like an elephant that could crush anything in its wake.

"Liftoff 3, eh?" The words were transmitted by the amber-haired manticore named Kit. Feeling came through the lines with the choppy sentence. She was focused and tense, the words were more an order than a question.

Kit transmitted the count and on three Herbert did his part and fired his set of thrusters to lift the top floors off the building.

It felt like jumping off a ledge in all the worst ways.

Visual sensors that were integrated with Herbert's mind showed layers of clouds passing by him. Gyroscopes that worked like his stomach fired wildly and wanted to make him vomit his lunch.

This building flew as well as an elephant.

Herbert ran through every diagnostic process at his disposal. The third of the ship under his control was run fine. Fat lot of help that was.

"Me ops green," Herbert reported to his partners. The sickness in his stomach came through. It'd be uncomfortable if the other manticores weren't feeling it as well.

"Want coaster ride no? Good fun," the blonde manticore, Melantha, said. The words came with plenty of excitement and humor. It masked her terror of lacking control of the ship. Manticores couldn't hide their feelings when transmitting like this, but she seemed to have a knack for piling plenty of emotion on top of the message.

Dismal trajectory predictions came faster than solutions. Herbert recalculated his thruster speeds to compensate for Melantha's lack of engine control. Kit did the same.

Wind rushed in the open hallway, now open to the cloudy sky of the Valley.

Buildings passed by the exterior visual sensors. Mandlestadt associates cursed as they used anything for a handle.

The most Kit and Herbert could do was slow their descent to the bottom of the Valley. It'd give everyone time to come to terms with their death, but that was all the pilots could do without Malantha's control.

"Online. Twin good," Melantha transmitted. The building bucked. A few associates lost grip of their handholds and tumbled to the ground. The pile of scrapped security bots flew out the open hallway and littered down to the Valley below.

Herbert and Kit adjusted their output to compensate for the new contribution. They had three districts to go and they were already off to a rough start.

***

"All perms, all thrust, yeah yeah!?" Herbert explained to Associate Yamamoto.

Yamamoto knelt in front of Herbert's dock with a silver flatworm cable running from his microfuser to the CPUs housed under the manticore's waist.

Herbert unwillingly transmitted his panicked yearning to be able to control the thrusters if Kit or Melantha went offline. He tried to give reams of technical specs to guide Yamamoto in this process.

The thin microfuser that ran into the associate's eye wasn't thick enough to hold all that.

"Damn manties. Can't understand them when they're like this," Associate Gomez complained. Her words came out slow. Herbert understood her just fine.

Yamamoto wasn't moving fast enough. He was likely a capable hacker but the microfuser speeds paled in comparison to manticore abilities.

The associate and manticore were a clutch and flywheel out of sync. And if they didn't get it together the whole building would stall out of the sky.

The speed at which things went from bad to worse only shocked Herbert because of how slowly it all happened.

He was used to lifts blowing up without any warning centimeters from his face. When that happened there was no time for recovery. You were at the bottom of the docks waiting for some Saints to separate your guts from scraps.

Right now, there was no shortage of explosions. Baumein commandos were firing missiles and lasers at the building.

Luckily, the exterior was designed to withstand it. A decision Baumein executives were likely regretting.

So far everyone inside the building was in one piece. Herbert couldn't say the same for those who fell out the open doorway after a hard bank to dodge enemy fire.

Baumein's fleet of security ships kept dropping commandos onto the roof. They occasionally made it into the building but were picked off by Associate Gomez or her coworkers before they could derail anything.

Unfortunately, the rate of the attacks increased as the ship approached Anodyze Tower. Despite the number of computers in Herbert's head he'd yet to find a way to land the ship in one piece. Kit and Melantha didn't have any ideas either.

All three manticores were running at full capacity. The rats and torso-less flesh legs that ran around the room assured Herbert he was at the edge of his abilities.

Mandlestadt could send out their own fleet of commands. But Yamamoto had explained it was company policy to only back up a mission if it was clear it'd be a success. Otherwise, the legal liability of a failed heist could bankrupt entire departments. If Mandlestadt stayed out of it though, their involvement was hard to prove and the destruction could be blamed on low-level mobsters.

It didn't take an executive to tell that this mission was corroded. Which meant that Herbert, and the other manticores, would lose his chance at a paycheck.

The associates on the mission were liable for much worth. They'd get demoted.

Assuming any of them made it out of this alive.

Herbert had a sewage of an idea.

He was currently processing the world around him at the speed of three manticores. He held independent choppy conversations with Kit and Melantha sharing trajectory calculation and which windows to fling open to get the commandos off their hull. Kit was trying to get the final blast door closed and Melantha was tracking the numerous Baumein ships that kept appearing.

But they were all having to split that attention with navigational calculations. It was slow and inefficient. And it'd be their literal downfall.

"Spin down, Yama' talk." Herbert communicated with his partners. He was hesitant about the trick and it came through on the wires.

There was a chance he could take a third of his mind and slow it down more than the others. After all, it already felt like he was three individual Herberts, just like he'd felt during the test.

"Bast'll kill ya," Kit cursed at him. Her emotions were full of confidence that he wouldn't be able to do it. Mixed in was fear that if he did then he wouldn't be able to pull himself out of it afterward, leaving the brunt of the work on her and Melantha.

Melantha transmitted the location of a new commando ship along with hysterical laughter and paranoid terror. Her eyes were bloodshot shifting around the room. Her long blonde hair was greasy with sweat and an unkempt mess.

Herbert couldn't imagine the terrors she saw. But felt like Kit was right to be concerned about taking on the brunt of the work. If Melantha overclocked, if any of them overclocked, the whole ship would drop out of the sky. All the more reason to slow down and talk with Yamamoto.

Slowing down one-third of his mind was most similar to lifting every noodle out of a soup simultaneously without leaving a ripple in the broth. Without a bank of spare computer processors, the calculations to do it would be impossible. Luckily Herbert had a cyberton of processing wired into his back.

He looked down at Yamamoto the iris of his 'hanced eye zoomed in and out unable to decide the right focal length.

Herbert closed his eyes. He still felt the shifting eyeball under the flesh of his eyelid. "I need permission to control all the thrusters instead of only a third of them," Herbert explained slowly to the hacker.

He opened his eyes to see if the man understood.

"There are limiters in here to keep any one manticore from gaining complete control over the..." Yamamoto's explanation was slow and dull and wasn't anything Herbert didn't already know from being part of the system.

Yamamoto's black hair cut in the shape of an upside-down bowl began to spin like it'd been knocked off the counter and landed on his head. Noodles spilled out of the black bowl. Herbert's enhanced eye could zoom in and observe each pore on the man's face. The pores opened up one by one to slurp up a noodle and clean the mess off the hacker's face.

"Manti!" Gomez shouted and followed it with the metallic clang of her chrome hands clapping.

"Unless you've got a way to make it look like one of you is three separate people I can't—"

Herbert's mind sped up he was still listening to Yamamoto's slow complaints about the impossibilities, he was still quickly calculating trajectories and receiving inputs from the other manticores. He also moved data around in front of him, assigned new network addresses to himself, and separated himself from himself like he was unpacking crates from a large shipping container.

It felt like a month's work. He was finished with it before Yamamoto had finished his explanation. And since he was communicating with the slower part of himself he could get back to the necessary work of driving the damn building.

"I just assigned three unique network IDs to myself," Herbert explained in his slow fleshy voice. "You can use that to give me navigational control."

"Elder's light," Yamamoto cursed in amazement.

Loud blasts echoed through Herbert's electronic eardrums. Gomez lowered her rifle as a bloody commando fell out of the open hallway he'd entered through.

"What happens if he overclocks?" Gomez asked.

"We drop out of the sky," Herbert responded.

Yamamoto assigned the permissions over to Herbert. It freed Kit and Melantha to focus on their tasks.

Kit closed the doorway cutting off any easy entrance for the commandos. Melantha gave Herbert precise locations of new fleet ships and their explosive projectiles. He dodged them letting them fly wild into the clouds or bystander buildings.

He could communicate with himself far easier than with two separate manticores. Rats still crawled up his back and through the cables from the ceiling. Flesh legs, amputated from their torsos, ran around. Gomez wasn't shooting at them so they must not have been a big threat.

Using the exterior cameras and streams of data Herbert navigated the building through the final sector of the city.

When it was clear that he'd be able to land the vehicle on the roof of the Anodyze building a swarm of Mandlestadt ships came to his defense. They buzzed about him like dockworkers eager for a shipment crate. But by now the aerial support was useless. Baumein wouldn't be getting the ship back today.

The top twelve floors, shaped like a pyramid, docked into the top of the Anodyze building. To Herbert, it felt like he was home like he had legs that were a hundred stories long. His millions of eyes, security cameras locked to the exterior of the building, looked out the the city around him.

He felt elevators move inside of him. Workers filed documents and ate lunch inside his floors. His three minds couldn't be merged, they each went their own separate direction within the building.

He'd gone beyond what any manticore could imagine. He was not merely the vehicle he drove. He was the building itself. A towering skyscraper filled with busy workers.

He could hear a million conversations, meetings, performance reviews, and back-office bribes.

He heard Kit shouting. "Get him out before he overclocks."

Her voice was slow using full words. It was so sloppy. Herbert could talk to himself without vocal cords.

The hiss of spinal connectors disengaging from his back echoed through his ears. All other conversations were muted. He no longer felt workers buzzing in his stomach. Bare legs and rats ran around the decorated Baumein room, but they faded out with time. Kit was lying back on a short gurney. Melantha was being lifted off her neural connector by Gomez, her eyes still bloodshot and darting around in paranoia.

A doctor in a white jacket pulled Herbert's forearms out of the silver dome they were connected to. The spinal connectors receded into the ceiling.

Herbert was disconnected from the building. The doctor lifted Herbert up from under his armpits.

Herbert felt something come up from his throat. The sudden halt of high-speed thinking was jarring. His flesh brain couldn't keep up, couldn't hold the three minds separate. It wasn't meant to do it.

Herbert had to eject a long sentence or regurgitate suppressed words.

He vomited on the doctor.

***

The pay was as good as promised. And as Kit and Herbert rode down the elevator they discussed the potential specs of their new parts. Melantha hadn't joined them, according to a doctor she needed further medical attention. Herbert didn't like the sound of it but surely her paycheck would cover whatever help she needed.

Before leaving Herbert had asked Gomez if there'd be more jobs like this, if the cap of the building would need to be moved again, and if they would be employing him or other manticores for the job the associate was quiet.

Gomez, always blunt, informed Herbert that Mandlestadt was promoting from within to find employees open to taking the position... amputations and all. Herbert had no doubt they'd find someone desperate enough for the job.

The second shift had just ended when Herbert found himself sloshing through the bottom of the Valley on his toe-less blue legs. Tavid would be off work, likely getting algae chili from the Saints. Herbert considered calling him to shop for 'hances or a new lift together.

But a lift, regardless of how new it was, would always pale in comparison to driving a building. Herbert would have to push himself to keep on top of the scoreboards. Split his mind and make himself sick, just to work to be on top.

He remembered the scruffy manticore that overclocked in front of him. He remembered the nauseating sensation of being in the Anodyze building, if only for a second.

Any 'hance or equipment he bought with the Mandlestadt paycheck would lock him into that future. Chain him to an inevitably short life that ended at the bottom of the docks, cleaned up by a Saint.

He might wind up down there anyway. But he could buy something that would make his short time in the Valley enjoyable.

Herbert called his friend and invited him to dinner.

"Should I meet you in the food court?" Tavid asked.

"No. Tonight I think we should enjoy a nice hot meal. Somewhere high up in the Valley."

Souvenir of the Valley

Thin metal blinds, bent and broken in multiple spots, did little to stop the neon colors of the billboard across the street from illuminating the bedroom. The screen was huge, blocking the view of at least ten stories of apartments. It flashed between bright reds, greens, and whites just often enough to keep Sophia awake.

She appreciated the visual nuisance. It kept her from falling asleep.

The ad was so big that lights were hardly needed to see the apartment, despite it being a hair past midnight. She wondered if it was better to have a view monopolized by the ever-changing billboard or to have your window blacked out completely, forced to stare at the back of the screen.

The apartment itself was a small studio. The bed she lay in sat behind a folding screen with a kitchenette on the other side. She doubted it was ever used.

The bed's thin sheets felt rough against Sophia's exposed skin. It was cheap standard-issue cloth that smelled musty. It held wet sweat against her back. She tried not to think of the other fluids it held onto.

The sheets likely hadn't been changed since her last appointment here. How hard was it to dispose of them in the laundry shoot? He'd get his deposit back. Buying a fresh pair from a vendor machine cost less than ten credits after the refund.

That was a whole lot easier than washing them by hand in the bathtub with your mother until they were thread-worn. Midtower residents didn't realize how good they had it.

The ceiling above her had exposed pipes striped in yellow, blue, and red depending on what they held. Occasionally the pipe's colors shifted as the billboard filtered through its ads. But the white light always returned to show the pipe's true colors.

She never understood if that industrial style was a cost-saving method or something 'glom associates considered stylish.

If her apartment had hardware exposed it meant something was broken. Usually bad enough that something needed to be done about it.

Sophia rolled over to face Harv who slept next to her taking shallow breaths. She pulled her long black hair out of her face draping it behind her shoulder. It'd need a good brushing before her next client.

She rearranged the lumpy pillow, another piece of standard-issue crap that was past its prime and rested her head near his. She leaned her chest on his right arm. The humid air of the night made her skin feel clammy where it touched his. If she was laying on his other side she'd get chills from leaning against the metal of his 'hanced arm.

Similar to Harv, her arms weren't the same. An intricate ivory tattoo ran from the tips of her right fingers down her body to her left toes wrapping around her torso like a beauty pageant sash.

Some compared the artwork to a circuit board, others thought it was a labyrinth. It was subtle on her pale skin, only able to be appreciated up close, with time. Time that didn't come cheap.

Harv slept lightly. He always fell asleep after her visits. It made him good about paying upfront, unlike some other customers. Sophia usually left quietly and let him be. So she almost felt bad having to wake him up tonight.

His hair was a short corporate flat top. The longer hair on top had felt like feathers to her hands when she was running them through earlier. The shaved sides were rough like sandpaper. She enjoyed the contrast.

Pieces of metal, holding small computers, were inset into his skin around his left eye. It was a common microfuser. It expanded his mind and enabled the operation of his 'hanced arm. The small lights inset in the metal above his cheekbone stayed dark and unactivated as he slept.

She placed her intricately tattooed hand on his chest. Short dark chest hairs, flat on their tip from a recent trimming, poked out of the flesh in the center of his chest. Clear evidence he was willing to do some preening for her.

Her long watchet-blue nails trimmed like an almond stroked his chest lightly. She disrupted the short hairs but they always folded back in place after she passed through. It seemed fitting.

Harv's leg moved towards her. She made room for him by placing her leg on top of his. That far under the covers trapped exceptionally hot and humid air. It caused her thigh to stick to his immediately. She regretted her positioning and wanted to shift herself. But it'd wake him up with a start, so she settled with the discomfort.

A few more strokes of his chest and the microfuser flashed to life. In a darker room, the lights would be blinding. In the light of the billboard, they were just another flash of color. Harv's eyes weren't open yet so Sophia closed hers.

She ran her fingers against his chest in precise patterns that would make it appear absent-minded. After a short moment, she felt his head turn to face her. She blinked her eyes open and looked at him.

"Sorry, I didn't mean to wake you," Harv said. "Just wanted to appreciate the merchandise before it disappeared."

Sophia let out a soft giggle. Harv wasn't the type of customer who appreciated an eye roll, even if he deserved it.

"It's fine," Sophia said, "I think I'll need to be going soon."

Harv's microfuser flashed. "I still have five minutes or so."

He pulled his hand away from his side and the movement tugged at Sophia's skin where she touched his. He placed his arm between her pillow and head then pulled her closer to him by pressing his arm against her spine.

It wasn't difficult to move her. She was a small woman. A feature most clients paid well for.

The computer in his eye gave him the ability to call up certain data: date, time, messages, even the score of the most recent sonicball match. If Sophia wanted that she'd need to use a hand terminal or an analog watch. She had plenty of those, beautiful timepieces gifted to her from clients over the years.

Harv could be lying about the time, probably was, but she couldn't call him on it without getting out of bed. And right now she needed the time.

"The merger tomorrow's going to be hell anyway," Harv said. "Glad I could book you before it."

"My pleasure," Sophia replied.

Harv's arm was long enough to reach her butt and he groped it almost absent-mindedly. That was not the direction Sophia needed this conversation to go.

She scooted her head down to rest it on his chest and reoriented her leg in the process finding something comfortable enough, considering the situation.

Now Harv's hand stroked the small of her back. She could feel him running his fingers over the tattoo on her left hip. The ivory tattoo left small ridges that only flesh hands, or extremely expensive bionics, could make out. Most clients found the texture intriguing. Which meant the tattoo was doing its job.

"The merger," Sophia put on her confused voice. "You said you were hitting Potter Tower?"

He'd gone on and on about the merger at the beginning of their session while she massaged knots from his shoulders and information from his mouth. But there was one necessary piece he'd been aloof about.

"Potter Tower," Harv laughed.

It shook his chest under Sophia's cheek.

"That's entry-level work. We're hitting Excella. It's a Baumein stronghold, has been for years. It's a four thousand footer with top security throughout."

"Oh really?" Sophia sounded surprised as if he hadn't repeated that info three other times this evening. "Security with guns and fancy metal enhancements?" She reached across his stomach and stroked his metal wrist. She didn't know if his model was nice enough to have sensors there. It likely didn't. But a gesture of fascination and admiration always played well with 'hanced businessmen.

"Oh, they have more than just guns hun. The reason it's been so hard to merge it over to us is their ALMS system. Even if we land a squad on every non-residential floor it'd just overload any unapproved microfusers in the area, making people like me go overclocked then braindead."

"But someone like me, without a microfuser, could walk in just fine."

"If you wanted to. But a ground-floor security bot could take you out no problem. Which would be a real shame." He stopped stroking her to squeeze the flesh of her hip with a small chuckle.

"So how are you going to get through the ARM system? I'd hate to lose you as a client." She squeezed his hip back, her hand could hardly fit around his hip. She doubted he minded.

"ALMS system, babe. And that's the genius of this merger. I convinced 19 Baumein associates to switch over for a promotion. And they haven't resigned yet, which means they're still approved to enter Excella."

He wasn't telling her anything she didn't already know. But he was talking which she appreciated.

"Nineteen is a lot," she sounded impressed, it was barely an act. Corporate allegiances in the Valley were hard to change, it'd put your whole family at risk of death or worse, unemployment. "How'd you find so many?"

"It's an exec family. Pardenzo or something like that. Everyone in the family from the grandfather down is upset because Baumein converted his granddaughter to a towermind. And he's been holding this grudge for a decade. Thanks to his family's status as generational execs they haven't had to resign and they're willing to take ALMS offline for us."

And that was the identifying info she needed. Barely cost her any overtime work. "And without the alarms, you can walk in without a problem? And I'll get to see you for our next appointment?"

"You bet babe, and I'll be much higher in the tower instead of this shit hole. Could start scheduling you every week with my raise."

"Sounds wonderful," she said in her most damsel-like voice. She kissed his chest, then rolled away from his arm and off the edge of the bed. It didn't matter how much bigger than you they were if you were one step ahead of them.

"I still got a few more minutes," Harv whined.

Sophia picked her galaxy blue silk gown up off the floor and wrapped it around her. Quick to get out of, and more importantly, quick to get into.

She pulled her hand terminal out of her pocket, the glass tablet showed the time was 12:33. She showed it to him; as if he needed the information.

"I can be quick," Harv said with a grin.

"You can't afford overtime yet, and you know none of my services are quick."

Resigned he reached for the vape on his nightstand and took a drag.

"But call me if you get that new apartment." She bent over to grab her purse that leaned against the foot of the bed. The loose neckline of the dress hung low.

It didn't reveal anything Harv hadn't already seen. But it held his attention nonetheless. Smoke, tinted by the red and green lights of the billboard, poured out of his mouth as his jaw hung open.

"At the very least get some new sheets," she added with more sass than she'd normally use for Harv's tastes.

She headed to the door swinging her hips. The hem of her dress fluttered around her thighs. The outfit didn't hide much because she understood marketing as well as any conglomerate exec.

***

Sophia's mouth was full. She tasted copper with hints of salt and umami that reminded her of the cheap algae soups she had when she was younger. But Sophia doubted the expensive 'hanced fingers in her mouth, or the Baumein executive they were attached to, had ever been near a dish that cheap.

This client, Veronica, always enjoyed pushing the sensors of her numerous 'hances to the limits. And Sophia was here to deliver that, along with some information. Veronica was paying handsomely for both. On an executive salary she could afford to, it was a corporate expense.

Veronica sat in a high-back armchair with wings that wrapped ever so slightly around her head. The arms were covered in thick padding that curled like a fresh cinnamon roll. They hung right in Sophia's eye line.

Cinnamon rolls were one of her favorite breakfast treats. Especially when baked fresh with white frosting drizzled on top. That was something worth salivating over.

Sophia didn't realize how much she was looking forward to breakfast. Her shift would be over in a few hours. She'd get home to sleep just after the hazy morning clouds evaporated out of the Valley.

The chair was upholstered in smooth white leather. It was unlikely to be the real stuff, but you never knew with a Baumein employee. They loved luxurious ornaments.

The room was a reflection of that. Lavish to the point of excess. It expressed Veronica's status in the company, along with a few of her personal obsessions.

Abstract paintings hung on the wall. Some reminded Sophia of insects she'd find crawling around the cheap apartments of her youth. Others she was confident were merely splotches of black paint.

The paintings surround the four-post bed. Each post of the bed was hand-carved wood. She'd observed those up close before, might wind up in a similar position tonight.

The comforter of the bed was as white as the armchair. Sophia knew the sheets under it were smooth silk. Veronica always used red sheets. When the fluffy white comforter was pulled back the red sheets always reminded Sophia of her mother skinning a stray cat for dinner as a kid.

Resting in fine silk wasn't Sophia's favorite, but she didn't mind rolling around in the material for a bit.

Plus she knew a maid-bot had replaced them this morning. Veronica could summon the helpful bot with a command in her microfuser. One of the many programs the executive used the computer for.

The most expensive items in the room, even if you assumed the armchair was genuine leather, stood sentry in front of the bed. Three bionic bodies in rose gold, dark metallic purple, and silver chrome were lined up against the wall. They were the centerpiece of the room. Technical masterpieces that outclassed hand carvings and fine paintings.

These torso-less shells were arms and legs attached to each other from armpit to hip with an interlocking metal sheet. The custom gap in the bodies fit Veronica's torso perfectly.

Each body suited a different purpose. From corporate boardrooms to espionage Veronica had the 'hance for any job. Presently the executive wore one with extra sensors imbedded in it. Perfectly suited to make the most out of an appointment with Sophia.

Veronica sat above Sophia, her head laid back in the armchair, eyes closed. Her dark brass forearm rested on the armrest of the chair. The servos in her fingers were unengaged, easily pushed around with Sophia's tongue. The sensors were still online, Veronica's soft hums were evidence of that.

Lacy white lingerie covered the little remaining flesh of Veronica's body. The white fabric popped against her rich sepia-brown skin. Veronica's torso was organic and curvy. Sophia would think the woman was beautiful even without payment.

Veronica had a full chest, the kind Sophia imagined she'd wind up with when she was growing up. It wasn't in the cards for her though. And Sophia, like everyone else from the bottom of the Valley, got by with what little she had.

Each appendage of Veronica's body was replaced with a 'hanced limb. Metallic legs with interlocking metal sheets on her bulky thighs reached up to her hip bone.

She wasn't hastily amputated from the waist down like a manticore. Veronica's procedure was done by a corporate doctor. She could afford the time and precision.

Time and precision that kept all necessary nerve endings intact allowing her to interface with the most advanced bionic sensors available. Which in turn made her well-suited for the profitable corporate espionage that Baumein paid handsomely for.

Sophia knelt on the ground in the red silky underwear that Veronica had just given her. It fit snuggly, the client knew her measurements well. She'd get to keep it if the garments survived the night.

Her black hair was pulled back in a neat bun, a few curls hung like window curtains around her eyes framing it nicely, in Sophia's opinion.

She'd taken an hour in a cheap hotel room after Harv's to clean up. It took a while to brush out the knots Harv had left in her hair. She then put no small amount of effort into her makeup which suited Veronica's tastes. To a Baumein executive, appearances were everything.

Which was why Sophia knelt in front of the woman, posing in such a subservient role. The executive likely couldn't see the power imbalance without it being played out overtly in front of her.

The client enjoyed acting out interrogations. With the right pay Sophia would give Harv's information over easily. But for a few extra creds, she was willing to cater to Veronica's fantasies.

The servos in Veronica's hand hummed to life. Her fingers brushed the hair out of Sophia's eyes, twirled around her cheek, and cupped her jaw. The palm of the metal hand felt cold on her chin.

"Where will your little Mandlestadt boyfriend be visiting tomorrow?" Veronica's tone was measured and deeper than normal.

Sophia blinked nervously and shifted her eyes towards the ground unable to move her head. "Ankor tower," she answered quietly in a tone that could only be picked up by 'hanced ears.

"Do not lie to me." Veronica pulled Sophia's jaw up to face her. "These hands are sensitive enough to feel any variations in your heartbeat. I'll know if you lie to me again, and you won't enjoy the consequences."

Veronica's cold fingertips squeezed Sophia's cheeks causing her lips to pucker. The touch was firm but not painful. Both women knew the 'hanced hands could do much more.

There were protections in place. Logs of where Sophia was, who she was with. In the old days sex worker unions would've protected her. But those had dissolved ages ago along with the rest of the unions in Galleria Valley.

Now it was up to the individual to take care of their protection. Some workers got picofusers, small microfusers that didn't blemish the face... as much. With those, you could embed small enhancements, a dentata, or silently request extraction in a pinch.

Sophia's father never allowed her to get even those enhancements. He was a crotchety deep doc fully aware of all the complications 'hances caused. He was happy to expose his customers, and himself, to the risks, but wouldn't approve of his daughter doing the same. She still resented him for it.

So she'd made the limitation her calling card, and now she couldn't afford to lose business by getting 'hances. High-profile executives like Veronica didn't consider marred skin on a partner desirable. Most executive spouses had no microfuser for this reason. Bare skin around the left eye announced your wealth. Unlike others in the Valley, you could afford to live without maximum productivity.

So Sophia turned to other means of protection. Ones that wouldn't necessarily save her life, but were strong enough to make her comfortable taking on high-profile clients. Mack, Sophia's partner, ran a crew that could get into the highest offices and most private of penthouses. Mack had inherited it from Mr. Louise and the gang's power terrified every employee short of board members.

Sophia trusted Veronica to follow the rules and limits outlined in their contract, as long as Sophia didn't mess with the executive's business. Unfortunately, tonight, Sophia needed to subtly push that limit. And if she wasn't careful Veronica would catch her and the executive would push back harder.

"He's going to Excella. Thirty minutes after first shift starts." Sophia waivered her voice nervously. She hoped her heartbeat played along as well. It'd ruin Veronica's immersion if it didn't. The woman's sense of touch was as crucial to her perception of the world as her eyes and ears.

Plus, Sophia needed to have control of her body for what was to come. For her own safety and the safety of others.

"How many?" Veronica's question came out fast and fiery.

"Three platoons are scheduled for the initial appointment. A dozen more are approved to join once it's clear the merger will go their way."

Mergers like this would get minimal support until it was guaranteed the mission was a success. Otherwise, the attacking conglomerate would be on the hook for damages to the offices, and apartments, and human lives. Expenses like that could bankrupt entire departments.

Everyone knew who ran the mergers. There were only two conglomerates in the Valley since the War of Acquisition. But that didn't mean it could be proven. And if it couldn't be proven, reparations for damage couldn't be collected.

Offices would recover. Both conglomerates had the funds to repair. It was simply the cost of doing business in the Valley. As for families caught in the crossfire... Sophia knew from experience they'd never get back on their feet.

"You know they won't make it long enough to use the backup," Veronica said. Her voice was smokey and confident.

"Yes, ma'am. I know."

Veronica's lips twisted into a smile. Sophia made a play to move away. The woman's metallic hands held her firmly in place. "You're not going anywhere anytime soon," she said.

Sophia's empty stomach was disappointed by this fact. She should've ordered room service at the hotel. Would've cost extra but it would've been worth it.

She couldn't be distracted now. There was work to do. Real work that'd benefit someone other than the Valley's conglomerate. Taking a deep breath Sophia did her best to focus.

"How do they plan to get past the ALMS system?" Veronica asked.

"They don't know about it," Sophia said. Her heart raced. She didn't work to calm it down. She was permitted evident falsehoods like this. It was part of the play. It also lulled Veronica into the security that she could pick up on Sophia's lies. Causing her to trust the woman when her heart was still even if it wasn't honest.

Weeks ago Mack had Sophia practice lying to an older model of the arms. In the back office of a low Valley bar, she lied to it to it until she was confident only the lies she wanted known would slip past.

She'd spent a decade controlling her expressions and emotions. She knew how to display only the emotions that customers wanted to see. That practice came in handy. But the sensors of the hands were delicate. Always able to spot her lies.

Until Sophia learned how to handle the appendage just right. Putting her back on familiar ground.

"Do you think I'm stupid?" The woman sounded genuinely miffed. Veronica pushed Sophia's head away and she fell backwards. She fell to the ground landing on the thin padding of a rug.

In one swift movement, Veronica leaped out of the chair and dragged Sophia off the ground by her bun. Veronica sat back in her chair and laid Sophia face down over her knees.

"I told you that you wouldn't like the consequences." The woman's left hand went to Sophia's butt, mostly bare under the red lingerie.

Sophia was more concerned about the woman's other hand. The cold metal ran up her spine, past the tattoo that crossed her back and rested between her shoulder blades. Inches from her heart, the sensors could pick up the finest variations in her pulse.

"What are they doing to get past the ALMS system?" Veronica asked again. She lifted her hand off of Sophia's butt, daring her to lie again.

"A Baumein exec family," Sophia blurted out nervously. She barely had to act. "Pardenzo is the grandfather's last name."

Veronica paused. After a moment Sophia turned to look at the woman. The executive's gaze was fixed across the room, the lights of her microfuser flashed quickly under her eye.

"Baumein doesn't employ anyone by that name," she said. She had a twisted grin like a tomcat about to catch a mouse. "But you're not lying. Or you're very good at lying." The executive looked down at Sophia and raised the unmarred eyebrow of her right eye, intrigued by the woman lying in front of her.

If Sophia didn't have a dozen other things on her mind that look would've made her melt into the woman's brass palms.

"Tell me more," Veronica's voice was calm, alluring, inviting. She rested her hand on Sophia's butt stroking the intricate tattoo that covered her left cheek. Trying to massage more details out of Sophia.

"The family is upset. Their daughter—granddaughter—was turned into a towermind. I don't know more."

"You sure?" Veronica's metal hand separated from Sophia's rear.

Sophia thought for a moment. Anything that would make her information legitimate and verifiable was necessary to get the pay. "There's 19 of them. That's all I know."

Veronica paused. Sophia stared at the hardwood floor in front of her. Following the grain in the wood to keep her heartbeat steady.

"Pascuzzo," Veronica said almost distracted. "Bellina Pascuzzo was hired as a towermind a decade ago. Her grandfather formally petitioned but her scores were too high not to employ her."

Sophia let out a sigh of relief and made it bigger than it needed to be. Veronica would appreciate her playing up her nerves.

"That's good information. Clever girl." Veronica stroked Sophia's bum and back as if she were rewarding a well-trained pet. "Anything else you need to get off your chest about the job?"

Sophia brought the information that Mack wanted her to pass along to the front of her mind. Then pushed it back. The more authentic she hid the information the better it would play out for her. Hopefully.

"No," Sophia made her voice tiny as she spoke.

Veronica landed a quick smack on her rear. Sophia let out a squeal. It'd startled her more than it hurt.

"I told you that you wouldn't like the consequences," Veronica said. "Now, tell me what else you know."

"The Syndicate is going to use the merger as cover," Sophia rushed the words out to make it sound like she was betraying Mack and their crew. "Hoping you'll divert forces away from the weapons cache next door at Potter Tower." Sophia breathed quickly. The cool metal hand on her back sent a shiver down her spine.

"They're coming in with heavy arms," Sophia added. She didn't say it like a threat. She offered the information like whipped cream on a waffle, an extra treat. And that part was true. When Mack showed up they'd have the weapons necessary to get the job done.

"Potter Tower doesn't have a weapon's cache," Veronica said as if she were presenting basic metrics at a board meeting.

Maybe it did, maybe it didn't. Sophia didn't know for sure. It was the line Mack told her to spill, so she did.

Sophia examined the wood grain and wondered if it was real. Unlikely. Some luxuries were beyond even Veronica's reach.

"Potter Tower does have a weapon's cache," Veronica corrected herself. She wasn't talking to Sophia. "A big cache. In such a small tower. What are they thinking?! We'll never move it in time."

Sophia quietly hummed with interest. The executive turned her attention to the woman in her lap. "Betraying your boss." She made a tsk sound with her tongue. "But it's not your fault. These hands can get a lot out of you."

Sophia let out a small whimper of shame and wriggled in Veronica's lap. She concealed the resentment at calling Mack her boss. No one ever understood their relationship, she doubted anyone ever would. It didn't matter to the task at hand.

Veronica's hand began to vibrate, massaging Sophia's back. "Now, let's see what else these hands can get out of you."

Sophia pressed her back against the hand. She wanted the stress of a long day's work out of her shoulders. But right now she had an appointment to finish.

***

Sophia buzzed into the penthouse with a pink box filled with a half dozen donuts balanced in her hand. She closed the door with her foot and placed the box on the counter. The great thing about working late was that it was easy to get the freshest donuts first thing in the morning.

"Mack, I'm back," she shouted down the hallway and towards the master bedroom. Her voice echoed off the hard granite surfaces of white rock with black swirls that covered the counters.

The penthouse wasn't as gaudy as Veronica's place but it was far finer than most of the places Sophia visited or slept.

Metal walls were cheap in the Valley because of the local mines. This penthouse was covered in them. A few were dented with bullet holes from the recent raid. Sophia had been threatening to get them repaired but Mack refused. They liked the damage for the same reason they liked leaving the scars from street fights on their skin. It reminded them to not get too comfortable in the Valley.

Sophia eyed the navy blue barstools. Faux leather wrapped around a padded surface. She wanted to sit down and rest her legs. Unfortunately, a seat wouldn't be comfortable due to how the rest of her appointment with Veronica.

"How'd it go?" Mack said coming out of the bedroom. They wore a tight black turtle neck with black canvas pants covered in countless pockets and loops. Two holsters hung on their belt, and the cyan grips of their guns poked out the back.

Their short neon green hair was slicked back with soft gel so it'd slip under a helmet and stay out of their eyes. Black eye shadow covered their eyelids.

Mack was dressed for an important merger, just like half the Valley this morning.

"Fine," Sophia said with a shrug. She pulled a jelly-filled donut out of the box for herself and rotated it to let Mack pick one.

Instead, Mack picked Sophia up and gave her a tight hug with a peck on the cheek. Sophia enjoyed being wrapped up in Mack's soft arms and broad shoulders. The hug was warm and reassuring. She leaned her head on Mack's shoulder for a moment of peace.

After a while but not nearly long enough Mack let go and grabbed a chocolate glazed donut and fit half of it in their mouth with one bite. "Veronica knows about the weapon's cache?" Mack's words were muffled by the flakey donut, but Sophia understood them just fine.

"Yup. Potter Tower. She was able to verify the info too. A very helpful touch that saved my ass."

"Thank the gamer kid you found the other day, he's the one who input the info." Mack finished the donut in a couple bites then headed for the coat closet.

"She thinks you're going after weapons there."

"Good," Mack said. "Execs always think we need more firepower. They'll be too busy guarding that I can get the hydroponic equipment slipped out the back easy."

"Mr. Louise trained them to think that way." The former Syndicate boss couldn't get enough. Couldn't give back to the Valley that raised him up. Couldn't see Mack sneak up behind him so they could inherit the Syndicate.

"He was no better than the execs," Mack grumbled. "But I'll make the most of it," Mack said with a smile.

"You always do." Sophia took a few more bites of her donut finishing it off as Mack pulled a shotgun out of the back of the closet. "Good luck. And be safe," she said.

Mack slung a bulletproof vest over one shoulder and pulled out a riot helmet from the top shelf. "If everything goes well I'll be back by lunch."

"If you're going to be home that early don't wake me up." Sophia licked the icing and jam off her tattooed fingertips.

"No promises," Mack said with a wink. They shrugged the bulletproof vest over their other shoulder.

Sophia rolled her eyes and headed to bed. This penthouse was high up in the Valley and far from any of her clients. She didn't have to worry about veiling her emotions here. She yawned unabashedly as Mack closed the door behind them.

She fell back into the plush bed, sheets unmade from Mack's night in it. The pillows still smelled like their partner's sandalwood shampoo.

It'd been a rough night for her. Most of the Valley was about to have a rough morning. It was impossible not to get caught up in the rush of the Valley.

Even if you didn't want to be a part of it it'd still blow through your door or window. Cripple your mother and arrest your father for unlicensed medical procedures.

Sophia knew she had to get wrapped up in it. Mack knew it even better. So she partnered with the mob boss and made the most of it.

Today the Syndicate would get hydroponic equipment deeper into the Valley. Hopefully into the hands of people who'd share the bounty, instead of selling its harvest with inflated margins.

People could barely work on algae stew and certainly didn't have the energy to fight back with empty bellies and malnutritioned kids at home.

Sophia rolled onto her stomach, curled up with a pillow, and fell asleep, trying not to dream about mergers past. She tried to dream about the good this merger might bring.

Mack's Merger

Mack hid for cover behind the bright yellow-wheeled forklift in the dock of the hydroponics level in Excella Tower. They were taking fire from the tower's security bots. Standard procedure for responding to non-Baumein personnel.

The next step would be sending in a group of 'hanced security agents. Specially trained associates with the latest enhancements installed. On a normal day.

Luckily, today wasn't normal. The merger had started thirty minutes ago and Mandlestadt forces were keeping the security agents of Excella Tower busy. No one would spare a thought for Mack and their team. Which is exactly what Mack wanted.

Squatting for cover behind the forklift Mack was weighed down by their body armor, headgear, and side arms. A few knives, some for throwing others for close combat were strapped to their body armor. The strap of the shotgun cut into their neck. The discomfort was a reassuring reminder that the tool was there if they needed it.

The shotgun was custom-made for Mack. Top of the line, by Valley standards, able to hold a few dozen rounds of different types. Ranging from scattershot to slugs to a few other special types.

With a microfuser the operator could change the round with a thought, Mack didn't have that luxury. So a dial was embedded above the trigger so they could scroll through the options with their thumb.

Expensive in the short term, but the cost of being dependent on a microfuser was more than Mack wanted to pay.

The dock looked like a parking lot for giants. Hovertrucks towered over Mack each cab had a cockpit the size of a sleeping pod. The engines poked out like the snout of a dog, heavily duty nuclear reactors that would carry the food grown on this level out to surrounding towers with ease.

And soon Mack would be using the trucks to carry out a few hydroponic machines of their own. Once Dasco hacked into the armored door of the hydroponics chamber. Right now the old hacker had a silver flatworm cable running from the microfuser on his left cheek to the door's interface.

His body armor was beaten and ragged. The shoulder straps were tattered and the bulletproof weave had a few splotches on it from previous gunfights. But Dasco refused to retire the vest despite Mack offering him a fresh one this morning.

He'd said the new ones uncomfortably cut under his arms and were too tight around his waist. The hacker was more interested in being comfortable than protected. Same reason why he didn't wear a helmet, he didn't like the way it rubbed on the bald part of his head or how it matted the hair around his ears and neck.

And that stupid sense of comfort was the reason he sat crosslegged in a battle zone, eyes glazed over and focused on the horizon. Dasco hadn't been beating on the door's code long. But it was still longer than Mack wanted to spend cooped up in this shooting gallery with security bots.

Although Phlox was doing a good job setting up auto turrets and taking down each new wave of security bots that came in the door. Her vest fit snugly over her broad metal shoulder. Mack wouldn't be surprised if Phlox used the proceeds from this job to cover the rest of her chest in bionics or start upgrading her legs.

The woman was hellbent on upgrading everything she could. Always had been even back when they dated as two young criminals climbing the ranks of Mr. Louise's gang. Phlox never understood Mack's disinterest in 'hances and her inability to fathom Mack's preference led to a breakup and now an uneasy working relationship.

But Phlox was one of the best, just like Dasco, just like Napalm who'd gotten them into the dock, around the swarms of Mandlestadt and Baumein ships. Landed in the garage without a single bullet hole in his precious neon green convertible.

And if Dasco didn't get through the door soon then they'd be using that same convertible to ditch this scene.

The repetitive machine gun fire from Phlox's auto turrets echoed through the room as three security bots, spindly black humanoids with guns for hands, walked into the dock from a concealed door.

Mack's right hand rested on their pistol holstered under their arm. Their other hand looked at their hand terminal as Dasco updated the team on his progress. As always Napalm was flooding the chat with messages about how they'd need to ditch soon. Leave it to an elevator to focus on escape.

The message came through first but Mack's ear's picked up on the hiss of the door lifting immediately. The reinforced door lifted up on vertical tracks. Before it was above waist height Phlox slid under the door. It always shocked Mack how graceful and quick the enhanced arms could move despite looking so bulky and slow.

Phlox would eliminate any threats on that side of the door before Mack and the rest made it through.

Dasco disconnected from the door's entry panel, the flatworm cable receding into his cheek like a long thin tongue.

"All clear," Phlox said. It was a subvocal command that could only be heard through Mack's earpiece. Everyone else got the message directly to their auditory cortex through the microfuser.

Napalm came out of hiding from behind some massive hover-truck, his bright red pompadour hair would've required a custom helmet to protect, so he didn't wear anything but blocky silver glasses.

Mack's partner Sophia was less worried about her looks than everyone on this crew. It was a liability, but it was also a fight Mack didn't want to get into today.

Mack slung the shotgun over their shoulder and entered the hydroponic room, hugging the wall in the process. Dasco and Napalm hugged the opposite wall.

Mack didn't like what they saw.

Dasco filled the chat with curses while Napalm asked a dozen questions.

The white room was the size of a sonicball gymnasium. Instead of court markings and goalposts, the floor was lined with red, blue, and green dashed lines that directed robots and forklifts.

The colorful pathways outlined a three-by-three grid. In the center of the grid's cells, there should have been hydroponic vats. Big plexiglass containers with dark green algae growing in them. Filters and nutrient dispensers should've been humming away feeding each vat they were strapped to.

The room wasn't empty, but the meat was stripped from the carcass. Large fans hummed above Mack's head moving humid air through the large room. A few standing terminals lined the walls and would've been used to monitor the vats if they weren't missing. Pallets stacked with bags of seeds and nutrients that would be fed into the vats were scattered throughout the colored paths.

A few doors that opened to hallways, elevators, or bot chambers were marked out in yellow and black trim. Mack would have to keep an eye on those. They were closed now, and it was a busy day, but someone, or something, could come through at any moment.

Phlox had her work cut out for her securing the room. Only one Baumein employee was in the room. He stood in the center of the vat grid, unarmed in a black shirt and tan rubber overalls. Waste management was stenciled on the front of the overalls.

His silver 'hanced arms were dented from bullets and the biceps were missing a few panels. The arms were raised above his head in surrender. Phlox lazily held him at gunpoint, waiting to hear what Mack's next order would be.

"Where the hell are the hydroponic vats?" Mack asked aloud. They didn't have the hardware to subvocalize to the chat. And the question wasn't worth concealing from this janitor.

Dasco connected his microfuser to one of the standing terminals that lined the room to get Mack some answers.

"They were removed yesterday," the janitor replied.

Mack lumbered through the room ignoring the pathways marked out on the ground. Their boots clunked on the warehouse floor with every step. They slung their shotgun to their back, then stood eye to eye inches from the janitor.

Mack was big, even without the body armor and helmet. The janitor didn't flinch at the mob boss's approach. Which made Mack hesitant to believe he was truly a custodian.

"You knew we were coming?" Mack asked.

No one should've known. Even the crew was uninformed of the plan until this morning. Sophia didn't know every detail of Mack's plan. And the dozen or so people Mack hired to prepare the job over the past few weeks only knew enough to get their part done.

"The queen sent me to introduce you to her hive," the janitor said. "She knew if the vats were still here you wouldn't take her meeting."

Mack scoffed. They were tired of meeting executives who considered themselves royalty.

"And a janitor was her best ambassador?" Phlox asked. "Why not a few associate or some tin men with persuasive firepower? Then I'd have some fun."

"As a token of goodwill, she has loaded up a vat into the back of truck 411B. The fob is in the front pocket of my overalls." The servos in his right hand loudly creaked as he pointed down to his chest.

Mack pulled the plastic fob out, it looked like a stone smoothed by sewage water. They tossed the fob to Napalm ordering him to verify the information.

"Where are the other eight vats?" Mack asked Dasco.

"There's nothing. No work orders to move it. There's no trail at all," the hacker replied.

Baumein associates were creative but no level of bureaucracy could hide such a large job.

"The sewer rat is right," Napalm said over the comms. "There's a vat and two pallets of nutrients in the truck."

"Make sure the engine isn't wired to blow or some other booby trap," Mack replied.

They took a step back from the janitor, now more curious than frustrated. "Baumein execs are only interested in giving things away when it benefits them."

"The queen isn't an executive," the janitor replied. "And she works for Baumein against her will. She would like your help with that."

"And in return, we'll get the eight other vats?" Phlox asked.

"She hopes that she can give you far more than a few hydroponic vats," the janitor said. His arms were still above his head like he was a 'glom teen facing a badge for the first time. But his eyes were locked with Mack's. Confident and unwavering.

"If she doesn't want to be associated with Baumein then walk out the door. Apply to Mandlestadt. The Syndicate doesn't have room for people who can't help themselves."

"The queen is not in a position to walk out of Excella," the janitor said. "She's far too connected."

Mack shrugged. Sure, conglomerates made people feel locked in through contracts, threats, enhancements that required maintenance, or lavish lifestyles. But you could always walk away. It just might not be comfortable. Her previous statement still stood.

"Truck looks fine," Napalm said over the comms. "There's room for the car too."

One vat was a good start. There'd be more vats and opportunities to steal them elsewhere in the Valley.

"Let's load up and get out of here," Mack said.

Phlox, who'd been lazily holding their gun on the janitor, moved their wrist ever so slightly. Mack thought they were going to shoot the poor janitor, an uncharacteristically cruel move for the woman.

But Mack hadn't survived on the streets by ignoring idle movements.

Before everything added up Mack leapt at Phlox's 'hanced arm. The gun was pointed right above Mack's waist a moment later. They grappled with Phlox's metal wrist to make sure it didn't point toward any unarmored part of Mack's body.

Mack dug their thumb into the gap between Phlox's hand and forearm. They dug around to find a delicate servo arm or anything that might put Phlox at a disadvantage.

Phlox engaged her broad shoulders and tried to lift Mack. The 'hanced arms could only lift Mack a few inches off the ground. Mack wasn't some tiny fly that could be shooed away from old food scraps. Their weight was an asset, like 'hanced arms or overclocked micro-fusers.

Mack made the most of being lifted off the ground and wrapped their legs around Phlox's knee. Their thumb found a delicate servo in the wrist. They pushed against it, snapping the part off.

Phlox's metal hand went limp.

Mack kicked at Phlox's knee and the two fell to the ground, with Mack on top. The position was familiar, but Phlox was groping for a gun this time.

Mack ripped the gun out of the limp hand, stood up, and fired a round into Phlox's right leg.

Aiming the gun at the prone woman's face Mack asked, "What the hell was that?"

"You're too conservative. If we're going to make a dent in this Valley we need to grab as much as we can when we can."

"You sound like Mr. Louise," Mack said.

"I'm not the one in penthouses with whores," Phlox retaliated.

Mack stepped on Phlox's injured leg. She winced as blood began to pool on the clean warehouse floor.

"The Syndicate needs a leader who will seize opportunities presented to them," Phlox continued, strained. "Not someone who will make the most of the scraps that get dropped on the Valley floor."

Dasco stood a few feet away with a med kit. Napalm was back to hollering curses and questions on the comm chat, lobbying to take the truck and go.

Mack removed their foot from Phlox. With the tip of the gun, Mack gestured for Dasco to start bandaging her leg and administering pain meds.

The woman had been plotting Mack's demise since before Mr. Louise was usurped. Yet this unceremonious rebellion was not what Mack expected.

This was not a well-plotted coup. Dasco and Napalm would never take her side, they were seasoned vets of the Valley, not some easily swayed disenfranchised teen fallen down from corporate towers.

Phlox's outburst had made her point. Loud and clear.

Mack had acted out dozens of times. Was ignored or punished by Mr. Louise. Then he disappeared blind to Mack's plot.

The Syndicate was not—should not—be an unchanging monolith like the Valley's conglomerates.

Mack turned to the janitor who was watching Mack intently. He still had his hands in the air but his face had a small smile on it.

Without concealing their reluctance Mack said, "We'll take this queen's meeting."

An elevator dinged from the back wall of the room.

Dasco dropped the auto-IV with a clank and drew his sidearm. Phlox groaned and drew their second pistol, of course, they had a second pistol. Mack trained their gun at the elevator as well.

Slowly the elevator door slid open.

Mack knew this would be a bloodbath. The room was too exposed. The janitor would provide Mack cover for only a bit before—

The elevator cart was empty.

The janitor slowly lowered his arms. "The queen bee will meet with you in the basement."

***

The basement of Excella Tower was messier than some of the alleyways Mack used to sleep in. Florescent lights flickered above an array of desks. Each desk was littered with electronics, crystal tablets, and embedded terminals. The floor was covered in puddles of sludge that literally smelled like sewage.

It wasn't like Baumein to allow for so much chaos. The janitor, he'd introduced himself as Nikandr on the way down, was not doing his job. Although Mack quit believing he worked for waste management a while ago.

Rats scurried around the ground, their claws almost imperceptible, but Mack's unenhanced ears had spent years training to hear them, catch them, and roast them. Mack's stomach groaned at the thought of a meaty rat to snack on. Should've had more than one donut for breakfast.

The merger would be over soon, but it didn't look like they'd be out of the building by then. Which made taking this queen's meeting even more risky.

Phlox's metal arm weighed heavy on Mack's shoulders. The bare metal felt cold on their neck. Nikandr had Phlox's other arm over his neck helping the woman walk into the messy basement room. Dasco was too old and Napalm was too lean to help carry the injured woman.

Phlox limped along on her good leg, muttering unfocused curses.

A janitor that wasn't a janitor, a messy Baumein basement, and a queen that ruled from the bottom of the tower. Mack was concerned. This was not how the Valley worked.

Tower basements were well secured. If someone could access the basement of a tower they could escape the tower altogether. Or they had immense pull and privilege and wouldn't want to leave.

The rest of the overhead lights flickered on. Mack hated overhead lighting. It was harsh and unnaturally white. A far cry from the overcast streets they grew up on. Plus it always scarred away dinner.

The roaches and rats scurried into the dark crevices of the room. Mack wanted to follow suit but had to hold Phlox upright.

The light revealed how messy the room truly was. A sewer grate was leaning against the wall puddles of sludge led out of it. Likely the reason the janitor had the rubber overalls.

A small pile of sheets, a coil stove, and a few dirty pans were set up in a secluded corner of the basement, far from the sewer entrance. Mack had made, and lost, many similar urchin camps as a kid. But none this secluded.

The most remarkable centerpiece of the room was the vat.

It was, unfortunately, not a hydroponic vat. Instead of murky green water this cylindrical vat had transparent blue liquid with silver bubbles rapidly floating up near the edges. Wires ran out the top of the vat and connected neatly, the Baumein way, to the ceiling.

Inside of the vat was an enlarged human head. The wires connected from the ceiling to the scalp. The face's pores were the size of Mack's fingertips and there wasn't a single hair on the entire head. Its eyes were closed, but the brow was wrinkled like Sophia having a nightmare.

Lights flashed on and around the vat. Mack assumed that it worked like a microfuser and indicated the head was puzzling something out with the aid of countless processors.

Mack swallowed hard trying to keep their revulsion at bay. They'd spent their whole life avoiding registration, 'hances, and associations with any conglomerate. Dependence on them, on anyone in the Valley, would do more harm in the long run.

And this head, this towermind that controlled Excella Tower from the basement, was the epitome of Mack's lifelong pursuit.

The eyelids of the towermind opened. Brown eyes with flecks of emerald green looked down at Mack and the rest of their crew.

It was rare that Mack felt small. Which intensified their desire to scurry out of the room.

"Thank you for taking this meeting with me," the speakers at the base of the vat said. The head's mouth did not move but the eye shifted to each member of the crew that stood in front of it.

"You're the queen that Nikandr wanted us to meet?" Mack asked, unsure how much they wanted to trust a towermind that was literally programmed to serve the conglomerate that employed it.

If Mandlestadt succeeded with the merger there'd be commandos pouring bleach into the tank within the hour. It was easier than re-programming these things.

The sound of metal scraping against the concrete floor of the basement interrupted Mack's thoughts. Napalm placed the metal chair he'd dragged over behind Phlox who lowered herself onto it with Mack's help.

The hair on the back of Mack's neck still stood up, despite the removal of Phlox's cold metal arms. It should've felt like more weight was lifted off their shoulders, but Mack was still uneasy.

"My name is Bellina," the vat's speakers said. "I have been the towermind for Excella for the past sixteen years." The towermind smiled gently. "And, yes to my hive I am the queen."

Mack didn't know what royalty had to do with rashes but cut to the point. "Where are the remaining hydroponic vats? What do you want us to do for them?"

"This merger is not going to go well for Mandlestadt. I've made sure of it. I'm programmed to. However, I believe with your involvement it will go poorly for Baumein as well."

Mack had a hard time believing that. Things in the Valley always went well for one of the conglomerates. Associates, denizens of the Valley floor, and members of the Syndicate merely made the most of how things panned out.

"Which is why you lured us here," Mack concluded, "to stop us."

"It is one of the few things I'm allowed to do, yes," Bellina responded.

Mack slung the shotgun over their shoulder into their hands. The towermind was still some flesh and blood, and a few well-placed blasts would at least buy Mack time to escape.

The giant head closed its eyes, seeming to be resigned to its fate. The lights on the base of the vat flashed slowly.

Nikandr stood with arms crossed leaning against a messy desk. Phlox had taken Mack's cue and pointed her gun at him but the man didn't change his posture.

"Takin' us down here's a slow way to stop us," Dasco said. His speech was fast, almost incomprehensible.

Mack turned around to look at the hacker. Mack wasn't worried about the head sneaking up behind them.

Dasco sat cross-legged on top of a desk. Electronics were pushed to the side or the floor without care. A silver flatworm wire ran from his left eye to the terminal embedded inside the desk. Lights flashed on his microfuser and the terminal screen. His eyes were glazed over and focused on something kilometers away. It was the look of someone analyzing a cyberton of data as quickly as possible.

"She's created a subsidiary that's been delivering raw material to random apartments throughout this tower. There's enough work orders and purchase orders documented to keep anyone from asking questions. But my summarization bots can't find any linkage to a 'glom-level project.'"

"So it's a secret project that Baumein doesn't want on file," Mack said with a shrug.

"It's not," Nikandr said. "Excella has slowly been running less and less efficiently, it's why they were exposed for the merger today. Bell has made sure that she only does the bare minimum. Board members wouldn't trust Excella with anything critical because of the sub-par performance."

"Why not outright rebel?" Phlox asked, her gun still pointing at the janitor.

"She can't," Dasco said, leaving barely any space between the words. "A seawall o' procedures stop her from acting without Baumein benefit. Remarkably the subsidiary's covert enough it doesn't flag any of those procedures though."

"She must rebel within the current system in order to change the current system," Mack said. They were familiar with the approach, but uneasy that they had so much in common with something so computerized.

"Exactly," the speakers of the vat said. "It is taking everything in my mind to keep from calling a dozen squads of security bots down here."

"Why drag us down here anyway?" Napalm asked. "Could've told us this in the vat room where we had an easy escape."

"Couldn't," Dasco said. "Subsidiary operates solely out of the basement. Connecting it elsewhere exposes it to 'glom audit routines."

Mack turned to face the head. "What's the purpose of the subsidiary?" Mack asked.

Bellina closed her hazel eyes. Her forehead wrinkled causing small ripples on the surface of the vat's water.

Mack turned to Nikandr, shotgun still resting in their hands, "You know why she's doing this?"

"No one does, not even the hive members getting the equipment. They've contacted each other, but they don't know what to do next. And she won't tell anyone."

"Can't," Dasco said.

Mack looked at the hacker confused.

Slowly, but still faster than his normal speech, Dasco said, "She cannot tell them. She cannot rebel against Baumein. But she is. At least she's close to rebelling. She's created and exploited a rift in these limiting procedures. Just enough to get the ball rolling."

"If we finish what you've started we'll get the vat?" Mack asked the towermind.

The towermind opened her eyes and smiled.

Mack's terminal pinged in their pocket, the sound startled them and they dropped their gun. The strap caught it and dug into their neck.

Pulling the terminal out Mack saw the message that came through.

"This is a contract," Bellina said. "If you, Robin McCoy, provide nondescript services then Hive Mind Subsidiary will render equipment as payment."

The head was smart, it'd found one of Mack's many aliases. They signed it with a squiggle of their finger on the terminal's touch screen. A dumb gesture that 'glom types thought meant more than a handshake or a threat.

"Boss, did you read this contract?" Dasco asked. He sounded shocked. But that might have been the speed of his speech.

Mack didn't know how to read much more than a street sign. "It's got instructions on what to do next?" they asked.

"No," Dasco said. "The subsidiary is not giving us the nine vats."

Mack wasn't entirely surprised. The damn 'gloms were always looking to screw people over.

The flashing of Dasco's microfuser slowed down. His eyes focused on Mack's.

"Boss," he said slowly. "The terms say assets rendered as payment are the entirety of Excella Tower."

***

The elevator dinged and the doors began to slide open. It'd been a long ride up to this point in the tower. If the airspace was clear outside it'd be quicker to take a car. But the merger was wrapping up and there wasn't nearly enough chaos to hide behind.

Nikandr was the first to step off the elevator. He was apparently the most familiar with the penthouse the crew was visiting.

Penthouse was an understatement in Mack's opinion. The entire floor belonged to a single family. Mack was disgusted by the idea, especially knowing how many people slept on the streets or in coffin-sized pods with only a backpack full of gear to their name.

But this family had "earned" it. Their ancestors fought in the War of Acquisition and happened to choose to work for the winning conglomerate.

The reception lobby of the suite was shaped like an equilateral triangle. The elevator exited in one of the corners. Each of the three walls had large double doors made of wood or a synthetic approximation of wood.

The best cover in the wide-open room was the front desk. It was built into the floor and a large glass wall behind it with monitors mounted on it. Images of the family that lived here played in a slide show, the whole lot of them looked as corporate as could be. Men with microfusers and tight haircuts, women with clear faces, and expensive jewelry. Each kid was dressed in suits or dresses that were likely as restrictive as their lives.

The lobby also had some furniture. Black corporate couches that were made of right angles, were designed to be used for no longer than the five-minute waiting period. A glass coffee table shaped like a pill with a robust black plastic frame under it. A few small chairs that could be moved around the room were available for additional seating but Mack doubted the seats would be comfortable or last long in a gunfight.

Luckily, they weren't planning to wait around to be let in.

The whole lobby was an awful place to have a gunfight. Especially, if you were the one coming off the elevator. The corporate designers were good at that.

The towermind, Queen Bellina, had recommended they start their work on this level. Connect with a Hive member named Devin Hackborn.

On the ride up Dasco had taken a cross-legged seat in the back of the elevator cart and analyzed all the information he'd downloaded about the subsidiary. He was silent the whole ride, eyes focused on a non-existent horizon.

The only reason Mack didn't think he'd overclocked himself was that he was still sitting upright. And he was a professional. Professionals didn't overclock.

Napalm installed an exterior quadricep to Phlox's thigh. The brace was rickety. The connection was slow. But the temporary 'hance would get them through the afternoon.

Mack really wished that Phlox hadn't gotten her leg shot. Would make the rest of this day easier on the lot of them, in more ways than one.

But after this, Mack would make sure Phlox got to a deep doc to get a new leg, or two, installed.

Assuming the crew made it out of here alive.

Assuming they could help this towermind get to the bottom of its own plot. How in the world was this crew going to solve a puzzle even a towermind couldn't solve?

Then what? Receive a whole tower in payment. That was a lot to give an unregistered orphan from the bottom of the Valley.

A lot to inherit. Own. Be responsible for.

It made a bullet hole in the leg look pretty trivial.

Sure Robin McCoy wasn't a real person. Mack could shed the identity and responsibility if they wanted to. They'd merely scribbled a signature in a dirty basement room. Mack had gotten out of more irrevocable deals made in shadier places.

But if they shed this responsibility why not shed the rest? Step down from running the Syndicate. Break up with Sophia. Go back to being a bum sleeping in drafty alleyways.

Let the tower, every tower, everything in the damn Valley, be owned and run by a conglomerate. Mandlestadt. Baumein. It didn't matter. Both cared about the sewage more than the people.

Mack wasn't interested in living in that world. It was ridiculous to believe Galleria Valley would change. But it was also ridiculous to believe Mack, of all people, would wind up running the Syndicate.

Times change.

Mack made the best of it.

Phlox stepped off the elevator behind Nikandr. Mack followed holding the butt of their shotgun close to their shoulder. Dasco and Napalm followed quietly behind the group as the elevator doors slid shut behind them.

"Get us out of this lobby fast," Phlox told Nikandr.

He was leading them to one of the synthetic wood doors. The path was clever. He made sure to keep the few bits of furniture and reception desk between them and the room's other entrances. There'd at least be a few seconds to hide for cover if someone entered the room.

Once they arrived at the door Dasco wired into the keypad with his flatworm cable. Phlox moved furniture around slowly to make a defensive position.

It didn't take long for Dasco to open the door. The door chimed and began to slide open. Dasco let out an uncharacteristic curse and pulled out his pistol.

Before the door was fully open Mack had dashed behind a couch for cover. They rested their shotgun on the backrest and aimed it at the opening door.

Phlox began to catch on and dropped the furniture in their hands. Napalm and Nikandr were slow to respond. The best thing Mack could do for them was take care of whatever threat was about to come through the door.

The humanoid metal shape in the doorway had Mack almost relieved. One security bot wouldn't stand in their way. But the dark purple metal of the legs and arms was too gaudy to belong to a disposable bot.

The heavily 'hanced woman nearly had to duck under the doorframe. Almost all of her body was replaced with bionics.

Her uncovered legs were slender near the floor, loaded up with springy suspension that would let her take off like a bullet if needed. Her large thighs had dozens of interconnected accordion plates that protected the heavy-duty hydraulics underneath. Unlock Phlox's arms there'd be nowhere for Mack to dig in fingers to damage the fragile mechanics.

Her biceps had a similar look to her thighs but her forearm was surrounded with barrels like one of Sophia's expensive bracelets. Except this one was far more deadly.

There were enough guns there to take down an army. So many that there was no room for a hand or fingers.

Her obliques were reinforced with metal plates connecting the arms and legs. Phlox was a human with a few mechanical muscles embedded into her back. This woman looked more like a human dropped into a bot's body.

Her head and torso were the only biological parts of her body. Her chest was covered in tight-fitting body armor that looked like the scales of a lizard. Her face was a rosy sepia with merlot lipstick and purple eyeshadow.

Leave it to a Baumein executive to match their makeup to their 'hances.

Her left scalp had tight rows of braided black hair that interlaced around her microfuser. The rest of her hair was a cascade of tight ringlets almost long enough to reach her shoulders. Mack had worried they'd spent too long on their hair this morning, but compared to this woman Mack primped in a flash.

Mack recognized the executive as Veronica immediately. They wanted to put a few holes into the woman's bionics or biologics. The only thing stopping them from firing was the innocent woman who dangled in Veronica's arm.

The hostage was as unenhanced as Mack or Sophia. Dressed in a tight-fitting black sheath dress, her caramel blonde hair pulled up in a bun. She almost looked like a secretary, but no qualified secretary this high in the tower would lack a microfuser. Mack didn't recognize her from the lobby's slideshow of family pictures but the resemblance was unmistakable.

Mack spun the dial near their trigger finger to select a heavy-duty slug. The current scattershot setting would endanger the damsel and do little to Veronica's armor.

They aimed Veronica's large thighs and fired.

Veronica's microfuser processed the world faster than Mack could even imagine. The executive dashed out of the way of Mack's shot.

The low caliber rounds of the rest of the crew's side arms did little to the executive as she rushed up to Mack. The mob boss didn't hesitate to fire again but Veronica kicked the barrel of the gun to the side and the shot went wide.

Up close it was clear that Veronica's 'hances were made for the singular purpose of combat. There were no gaps between muscles that Mack could use to their advantage as they had in countless street fights before.

Standing on the couch looming over the mob boss, Veronica pointed her hand of firearms down at Mack.

It wasn't the first time Mack had looked down the barrel of a gun. But this was more than Mack was comfortable with.

But just like all those other times once again their opponent had made the mistake of getting too close. It was easy to underestimate someone without a microfuser.

Mack used the shotgun to push Veronica's arm high and leaped out of their kneeling position. They got under the executive's armpit and Mack's helmet thudded against the metal of Veronica's body. The blow did little damage to both of them but Mack's weight threw the Veronica off balance.

The exec's heavy 'hances were probably strong enough to lift Mack. But for a moment Mack had the upper hand.

Veronica fell back with a thud and let go of the woman in her arms.

Hitting the ground took the breath out of Mack but Veronica seemed unfazed. She was up in an instant. But Mack still clung to Veronica's arm and wrapped their legs to her torso.

Veronica's now free hand punched Mack in the side. Mack's body armor did everything it could to cushion the blow but the boss still cried out in pain.

Mack continued to grapple the right limb as it tried to twist back and get a clear shot at them. The body armor Mack wore would be useless at point blank.

Veronica took another jab at Mack's side. They stifled their cry this time, despite being confident the blow broke at least one rib.

Before Veronica could continue her beating Phlox arrived. Both of her metal arms grabbed Veronica's free hand that was wailing into Mack.

Phlox was familiar enough with Mack's tactics to know what her boss wanted. She kicked at Veronica's knees with her braced leg and took the exec to the ground again.

With the two of them on top of the executive there was not enough power in her legs to get up this time.

Mack drew their pistol from its shoulder holster. Firing the low-caliber weapon into the metal of Veronica's arm would do little good. Using one of their knives would do more damage to the blade than the arm. So Mack used the butt of their pistol to dent and damage every barrel on Veronica's right wrist.

It'd be a quicker repair than Mack's rib but it'd keep Veronica from being able to do much damage for now.

Phlox was going to work on the other side and the sound of metal clashing against metal with its scrapes and dings filled the room.

To someone as enhanced and wealthy as Veronica death held little problems. It was a mere reboot into a clone of a tin man's body. Mack could do more harm by damaging Veronica's property than her body.

Veronica unexpectedly twisted her legs in a double-jointed move that no normal human should be able to do. The executive hooked their legs around Mack's chest and scraped the boss off of her arm.

Pinned under the woman's metal legs Mack thrashed against them but the thighs were too heavily armored to care.

With Veronica's free arm, little more than a wad of expensive purple metal, she struck Phlox in her metal shoulders.

With a loud clang, Phlox fell over, and Veronica slipped her arm out of the woman's grasp.

The hydraulics next to Mack's head engaged with a hiss and the executive dashed up and to the elevator across the room.

Mack lay on the ground, able to watch the executives escape between the gap under the couch.

Dasco and Napalm continued to fire towards the elevator. The executive took cover behind the elevator's wall as the doors slid closed behind her.

Mack looked up at the metal tiles of the ceiling. Wondering why they ever trusted the towermind in the first place. The brain sent them into a trap. An ambush.

The whole crew was lucky to be alive.

And Mack knew they'd have another meeting with this exec. They began to catch their breath from the fight. The stinging ribs reminded them that one of them would be able to repair from this fight faster than the other.

***

Mack wondered how they'd missed the white-robed minister standing in the doorway in the midst of the shootout. He'd stood out like a cockroach on clean tile. Except unlike a cockroach he wasn't clever enough to scurry away.

The patchy red beard on his soft chin was unfortunately familiar to Mack. Although he didn't seem to recognize the mob boss under their helmet. He stood, near the doorway, unfazed by the entire situation. As if his position or his flowing robes could protect him from the gunfire.

Napalm held the minister at gunpoint, and Mack had confidence that this was an adversary the driver could handle. Nikandr tended to the damsel Veronica released as she escaped, they seemed to recognize each other, which made Mack even more suspicious that this was a trap.

Phlox stood over Mack offering a metal hand to help them up. With some quiet winces, Mack got to their feet. Dasco offered an Auto-IV of pain relievers and Mack rolled up their sleeve willing to take anything they could get to relieve the pain. Wishing they'd gotten their ribs replaced with titanium the last time they broke.

The suite behind the door was a living room kitchen combo. The living room had a glass coffee table in the center with a couch behind it.

The couch was decorated with a few bullet holes tying it in with the shot-up abstract paintings on the wall behind it. Two armchairs flanked the coffee table as well. The seating was well positioned and every spot gave a clear line of sight to all the room's doors.

Mack and the crew slowly shuffled inside and the main door locked behind them with a loud hiss of the hydraulic seal.

In the relative safety of the suite, Mack pulled their helmet off. Their green hair smelled like lavender shampoo and brine. It was wet with sweat and hung in front of their eyes, the stiff gel that held it back this morning had worn off.

Once in the room, Mack could get a better look at the kitchen. It had a brown granite island with leather-covered bar stools facing the counter. The counter, tucked away on the same wall as the main door was protected from the crossfire. It had a matching granite countertop and a dozen of world liquors lined the back wall. A small bar sink was inset furthest from the door and next to a fridge hummed away in the corner.

"Would anyone like some coffee or tea?" The unenhanced woman offered standing behind the island. Everyone in the room was keeping a suspicious eye on her except Nikandr. She may lack a microfuser but she could still pull out a gun from the cabinet. Instead, she pulled out a cast iron teapot decorated with an intricate dragon.

"I'd like some answers," Mack said as they sat down on an armchair a little too fast for their injuries. They poorly stifled a groan. "Who are you?"

"Devin Pascuzzo, this is my suite. Or was before my family transferred to work for Mandlestadt." Devin began to dose tea leaves into the teapot.

Baumein elites, always hospitable, even if you just shot up their couch. A Mandlestadt would be trying to trick you into a contract of reimbursement.

"Why was Veronica here? And the minister?" Mack asked gesturing to the white-robed man whom Napalm was tying up to the barstool. The fancy stool not only had a back but padded arms, far nicer than any stool in the deep Valley bars Mack ran.

Devin brought the tea to the coffee table, a sheet of crystal glass that hadn't shattered in the crossfire, and could probably take a few more shots like most executive furniture.

She poured a glass for everyone who'd followed Mack's lead and taken a seat on the couch.

Dasco was zoned out in some cyber world uninterested in the tea. Phlox and Nikandr sat on either side of him, their gaze shifting from the door to the tea to the minister, waiting for something unexpected to happen.

After serving the tea Devin took a crosslegged seat on a floor cushion, her back to the door. Mack was shocked she'd taken such an uncomfortable position when there was an empty armchair still available. Mack wasn't above sitting, or sleeping, on the ground. But wouldn't be comfortable with a door at their back.

"Veronica was here to execute my family," Devin finally answered after sipping the cup of tea she'd poured herself. "My father, grandfather, and husband fell back to my grandfather's conference room once the merger went south. Based on the gunshots coming from there it sounded like she was successful. "

Mack took a sip of tea now that Devin had some. If there were drugs in the drink they'd have to compete with the cocktail of pain relievers Dasco had injected earlier. The drink was piping hot and tasted almost like seaweed, a little salty and a little savory.

"You seem unconcerned with their deaths," Mack said, wondering if it was a professional act or if she was here because she was in on the plot.

"They had backups uploaded to Mandlestadt mainframes last night," Devin said. "They'll be rebooted into clones or tin men within the hour. My mother, sisters, and the kids without microfusers migrated to Mandlestadt safety last week, in preparation for the merger."

Mack shook their head. Even a meeting with death could be rescheduled with enough money.

"And the minister?" Mack turned to address the man now tied to the barstool. Napalm was rummaging through the kitchen's fridge for something to drink.

The minister looked at Mack, indignant and silent. Mack looked up at the ceiling and groaned in frustration. "The last thing I want to have to do today is torture you for information," they said patiently.

Mack looked back down across the room at the minister. Napalm had found a cold sour beer in the fridge and popped the aluminum can open with a loud hiss.

The minister looked firmly back at Mack, unconcerned with the threat. Mack unsheathed a large knife that was strapped to their chest. With the silver blade between their fingers, they passed the knife to Phlox who'd already stood up.

Phlox inspected the knife as she walked over to the minister. The curved blade didn't look as big in her metal hands, but the minister's eyes got wider as the knife got closer.

"Boss did this to me." She pointed the tip of the knife at the bandage around her thigh. "Just imagine what they'll do to someone who doesn't work for 'em."

The minister tried to keep a straight face as Phlox placed the knife on the first knuckle of his pinky finger, but he wasn't nearly as in control of his emotions as Devin.

The knife was sharp. Mack had touched up the edge two days ago.

With a single nod of their head, it sliced through the minister's finger.

He hollered in pain followed by some amateur curses and then threats. "Injuring a Central System Minister is punishable—"

"Shut up," Phlox said as she placed the blade on the second knuckle of his finger.

Blood had run down the arm of the barstool and stained the lower part of the robe that covered his legs.

"Something easy," Mack said sipping the last of their tea. They stifled a wince as they leaned forward to place the cup on the glass table. Devin refilled it, unconcerned by the violence behind her.

"What's your name?" Mack asked.

"Minister Liesel. Twelfth sector, third division…" he sputtered out some more jargon that was unimportant to Mack who cut him off with the wave of their hand.

"You grew up here?" Mack said.

He nodded.

"You left. Not cheap or easy to do. You became a minister and decided to come back to this sewage pit." Mack shook their head almost disappointed.

"I did. I came back to clean up the crime in the Valley. The plague you and Mr. Louise spread across this place."

Mack chuckled. "You were raised rich enough to hear the propaganda, but not rich enough to be taught it was a lie."

"I've seen the statistics that the conglomerates send the Central System. Your gang activities cost lives and damage equipment that needs to be shipped off world. You're endangering life from expanding into the cosmos, and the Elders can't abide that."

"'Gloms are endangering life from surviving in the Valley! If I could send out statistics your Elders would piss their white robes,"

Mack said. "This merger alone has likely killed more people than the Syndicate does in a quarter."

They knew they weren't going to be able to convince the minister with just words. He wanted data. Mack pulled out their terminal and looked for a packet of data related to Clarvo they'd received recently.

"And you're at the center of it," Liesel said, his accusation dripped with disdain. "Running through this tower. Raiding this suite for god knows what. Injuring a conglomerate executive."

"I'm on the fringes at best," Mack scoffed. "I am only here because the towermind sent me. And I'm regretting listening to that floating head that thinks it's a queen bee. You want to see who's the bad guy? Look at this."

Mack threw their hand terminal with Clarvo data at Phlox.

Phlox caught it the metal of the terminal clinking on her metal hands.

"You'll let me go immediately if you know what's good for you," Liesel said.

Mack had a few broken ribs to vouch for the fact they in fact did not know what was good for them.

Nonetheless, Liesel looked at the data on the terminal getting a little bit of blood on the back of it.

"You mentioned a queen bee," Devin said politely.

Mack grunted in acknowledgment. They needed a rest and this day wasn't nearly close enough to being over.

"I am part of a group of people receiving packages marked with a queen bee," Devin said. "We call ourselves the Hive Mind."

"Good," Mack said, glad that this visit to the top of the tower was going to go somewhere. "You've been building something for her?"

"A few things. But we don't know what it does. Did she tell you?"

"Dasco's got a few files on the Hive Mind Subsidiary." Mack jabbed their thumb at the zoned-out hacker sitting cross-legged on the couch. "But show us what you've got so far."

Devin stood up gracefully from her position on the floor. Mack was less graceful, letting out more groans than they wanted to.

"We have a med-bay," Devin said. "I was going to use it to install a microfuser. But it could stitch up some bullet holes if it needed to."

"I need more than a few stitches. Can it do a new set of ribs," Mack said with a painful chuckle.

"It can," Devin said. Her voice was absent of any hint of a joke.

"A new ribcage could be good for you boss," Phlox said wiping the blade of the knife on Liesel's sleeve and handing it back to Mack as they walked by.

"I'm not interested," Mack said flatly. "And we don't have time."

"It's a top-of-the-line machine," Devin said. "Grandfather imported it from a company that used it off-world in combat zones. It's designed to get troops back to the frontlines and save on manufacturing new clones."

"I'm not interested," Mack said with a scowl.

"Of course," Devin said. And if she was hurt by Mack's bluntness she hid it behind a smile. "I'll show you the equipment the queen sent."

Mack followed Devin towards a small door off the side of the kitchen. Phlox and Nikandr followed close behind. When Devin reached for the doorknob the lights in the room went out.

The interior room had no windows so the only light was the flashing of the crew's microfusers. Dasco's microfuser flashed like a dance floor, he seemed unfazed by the darkness. Familiarly absorbed in his own world.

The rest of the crew's microfusers flashed at a slow melodic tempo. Phlox's eyes began to glow a yellow-green as her night vision 'hances kicked in.

Mack pulled their sidearm out from under their armpit, the one that hadn't been used to bash in Veronica's weapons. They turned on the flashlight at the tip of the gun and pointed it at Devin and Nikandr, both of whom shielded their eyes.

They were as taken aback by the stunt as anyone on the crew. Mack was still concerned this was a trap.

"Minister's stationary," Phlox said.

"Doors will fail open," Nikandr said, his eyes glowed a yellow-green as well. "There could be an army coming through that door any minute."

"There won't be," Dasco said. His microfuser had slowed down and he spoke at a normal rate. "The entire building just lost power."

***

At a young age, Mack learned that living without any enhancements meant they had to be prepared for any and all eventualities. This was a sentiment that Devin, the unenhanced daughter of a powerful family of senior executives, didn't seem to grasp. Napalm and Dasco also lacked any solutions for operating in the dark, despite their microfusers.

If Mack's crew was representative of the tower as a whole every floor to the base of the Valley would be in utter chaos. Unfortunately, Mack's crew was more professional than the average tower citizen.

But it wasn't surprising that no one prepared for a blackout. Towers don't lose power. They are wired into the generators at the base of the

Valley. Fueled by the planet's mines which were operated by machines that have been in place for thousands of years.

Even in a merger Mandlestadt and Baumein wouldn't sabotage those without hurting themselves. And if Excella Tower was disconnected from the power plants it'd be back online in a moment.

For the past twenty minutes, Nikandr had followed Devin like a stray dog begging for scraps. Devin had searched her entire suite for some sort of light source without any luck.

As for Mack's crew, Napalm had mastered the path from the bar to the fridge in the dark and was keeping the minister company at the bar. Dasco spent the time explaining what he'd learned about the subsidiary to Mack and Phlox who refused to let their limited vision stray too far from the front door.

"The power likely didn't affect Bellina too much," Dasco said. He was seated cross-legged on the couch.

Considering the entire job was now dependent on the towermind Mack was concerned about its wellbeing, even if they didn't trust the mind.

"Our brains use up a disproportionate amount of the calories we consume in a day," Dasco continued explaining. "And Bellina is just a head and a big one at that. So she needs a lot of nutrients. There are backup batteries to keep her tank filled with nutrients for at least a week. But after those ten days are up, she'll starve."

Mack figured if the tower was blacked out for a whole ten-day week there'd be bigger problems on Baumein's plate than a towermind starving.

"No way the power stays out for another ten minutes, let alone ten days," Phlox said, their eyes still yellow-green in the dark.

Mack remembered her saying something ten minutes ago. But eventually, Phlox would be right. Power would come back on, and there'd be an army of security bots, or worse, for them to fight off.

"However, the nutrients she needs is the least of our concerns," Dasco continued. "She is wired into the building, the majority of her mind is computers that run in the supercooled basement floors around her. This power outage is effectively a lobotomy."

"So it's like her microfuser blew," Phlox said. "No big deal. I operated fine before I got mine installed I'll operate fine until I can get it replaced."

Mack was still operating fine without one, all these years later. But they still wouldn't like part of their mind disappearing.

"You'd operate without arms," Dasco pointed out.

That was exactly the reason Mack didn't want 'hances. You were flat-footed if they failed.

"Sure," Phlox said, unconcerned by the prospect of being an amputee. "But Bellina doesn't have a body, or anywhere to go. If she's mostly computer then this will just feel like a reboot."

"She has a body," Dasco said. "It's this entire tower. And it's not a reboot because her brain is still operating. She's just void of any sensory input. The blackout she's experiencing is far worse than us operating by the light of Mack's pistol."

A pistol whose battery was draining every minute Devin didn't come back with some other light source.

"So the towermind wasn't the one who shut down the power?" Mack suggested. They'd hoped that since it was unlikely to be the 'gloms that did this it was part of the towermind's plan, and Mack could make the best of it.

"Maybe Baumein found out she was plotting against them," Phlox said. "This would be a perfect opportunity to take her offline."

"It's a very conspicuous solution to the problem," Dasco replied. "'Gloms have been disposing of towerminds for centuries, without blacking out towers."

As much as Baumein cared about appearances a blacked-out tower was not a good look for them. Especially after an attempted Mandlestadt merger.

"And do we know if it's only Excella that's down?" Mack asked.

Nikandr entered the room, his green eyes the only thing that Mack could see in that direction. "Based on the view out the master bedroom window every tower we can see is still operating."

"A last thrash of Mandlestadt rebellion?" Phlox offered. "Salty like seawater since they lost the merger."

"Sets a bad precedent, professionally," Devin answered as she walked up to the glass coffee table where Mack's pistol threw some light in the direction of the door. If anyone in the room understood inter-conglomerate negotiations it was her.

She placed down three candles and lit them with an antique metal lighter. Fancy execs didn't have anything practical like a torch, but had plenty of fancy archaic junk.

The yellow candlelight flickered like a microfuser processing thoughts. It illuminated everyone's face from strange angles. It lit up parts of the kitchen, including the minister who was still tied to the barstool, although his finger had quit bleeding. In the candlelight, it almost looked like he hadn't lost it at all. But that was just the poor lighting.

The candlelight was bright enough to reach the doorway, and Mack turned off the flashlight on their gun and holstered it.

"As uncomfortable as this blackout would be for her, I think Bellina is the most likely suspect," Dasco said. "The subsidiary files don't prove—"

"Did you just say, Bellina?" Devin cut him off. Her voice was not accusatory but confused.

"I thought you knew," Dasco said.

Mack sure wasn't clear on the situation. And they hated moments like this where someone's access to a microfuser and the perfect memory it brought trumped their own.

"Your sister, Bellina, is the towermind for Excella," Dasco explained. "She was assigned here under Board Member Hoffman's experimental program. She underperformed for his program but was left intact as a towermind."

"Which is why Grandpa worked so hard to get the transfer out of Crest Tower," Devin said. She spoke like a child suddenly connecting the dots of their parent's puzzle. "He would've been far more successful with a merger in Crest. There were generationally loyal families there."

"How does a towermind have the ability to take a make a tower blackout?" Mack asked eager to return to the task at hand. The candles had started to put off a pleasant citrus smell that reminded them of Sophia, the person they really wanted to return to.

"From a technical standpoint it's fairly simple," Dasco said. "Towerminds can control all aspects of their tower. But she'd need a good reason to shut the whole place down. And an even better one to keep it down, since it'd be in the best interest of Baumein to get this place up and running immediately."

"Bell could always drag her feet when she wanted to," Devin said.

"Towerminds aren't as independent as you and me," Dasco said. "They're integrated into the tower, pre-programmed not to rebel. She's not doing it through any force of willpower. There must be a thorn in her side forcing her to keep it down. Maybe something the Mandlestadts inserted during the merger."

"No, it wasn't them," Nikandr said. To Mack's ears, he almost sounded ashamed. "I did it a few weeks ago. I found a security assessment report on a basement computer. Bell had generated it. But instead of sending it to an exec, she left it running on a computer near my bed. Along with the equipment needed to execute it. So I followed the report's instructions."

"She told you to just casually proceed with corporate espionage in her own tower?" Phlox asked, shocked.

It was clear to Mack that Phlox, ever stubborn, still didn't understand the towermind's situation.

"She didn't tell me to do anything. She couldn't. But I have no allegiance to the 'gloms. If the report was left there for me to find she meant for me to do something with it."

"So you know how to undo this blackout?" Devin asked.

"I do. And I heard Dasco talk about how uncomfortable this is for her from the other room," Nikandr said. Mack didn't doubt that he had some 'hanced eardrums in that thick skull of his. "I'm going to remove the devices immediately."

He moved towards the door but Mack got in his way moving by the light of the citrus-scented candles.

"Don't be an idiot," Mack said. They put a hand on his shoulder to hold him back.

"My only allegiance is to Bellina," Nikandr said. His metal arm pushed Mack's hand away without a care. "I got her into this mess of being a towermind, I'm not going to make her suffer more."

"She wanted this tower to go black for a reason," Mack explained. Even if Nikandr wasn't loyal to a conglomerate he was still as stubborn as a young 'glom associate. "Immediately undoing it would undermine her intentions and her suffering. We're better off figuring out how she wanted us to use this blackout."

Nikandr groaned. "I'm not willing to make her suffer more than a day."

"The residents of this tower will be in chaos before sunrise if this tower stays black that long," Mack agreed.

Mack turned to Dasco, with the warm candlelight on his face and his cross-legged seated position he looked like a monk. "You said one of the subsidiary members built a battery array?"

"Yeah, Kiran did," Devin reported. "I met him yesterday when he delivered the antennas I needed."

"We've got Devin with an antenna array," Dasco said. "Kiran with a battery bank. Amaranth has a generator. The twins Quai and Lewd both built a massive computer with no operating system on it. And W Y K Y was given three dozen fake work orders to install transmission lines throughout Excella but they don't connect to anything."

"That's the whole hive," Devin confirmed. "And you pronounce W Y K Y as Vicki. She was in here two weeks ago running lines to the guest room."

"The guest room doesn't happen to be where your antenna array is?" Mack asked.

"It is," Devin said. "But Wyky's work order didn't say anything about hooking it up to the antennas. Plus the assembly of my device wasn't complete."

"Of course, her work order didn't say anything about hooking it up," Mack said. Leave it to an executive's daughter to not understand the idea of working against a system from inside it. "If these devices are supposed to undermine Baumein the towermind wouldn't be able to admit it."

"Is Wyky a spider with old-school metal eyes," Nikandr asked Devin.

"Yeah, went blind in a dock accident and couldn't afford decent 'hances. So now she goes by Wyky with no i's."

"She was in the basement last week," Nikandr said. "Scared the sewage out of me. Thought I was gonna be evicted by some Baumein scientist."

Mack could relate to that feeling, although it'd take more than a scientist for them to give up such a good hiding.

"Wyky has a work order for every single hive member's apartment," Dasco said. "So I guess that explains what they connect to."

"So we have a computer that runs independent of Excella's grid. Convenient, considering Excella doesn't have any power," Mack said. "And it can plug into our towermind since Wyky ran wires down there."

"But without an operating system for the computer it's just expensive circuitry," Dasco said. "Bellina won't be able to interface with it."

A chuckle came from the kitchen, but it wasn't Napalm.

The candlelight flickered on his white robes. The minister had a smile on his face that seemed to twist in the candlelight.

"What's so funny," Mack asked, wondering if he'd be laughing after losing another finger.

"Just the way things come back around. If you need an operating system that can interface with a towermind, I'm your guy."

***

The twins Quai and Lewd let Mack and the minister into their messy apartment without a question, and likely without a second thought. A few questions from Mack and it was clear that the computer wasn't the only thing in this apartment running without an operating system. The twins were slower than cold sewage running through thin pipes.

They sat on their couch, a dozen empty boxes of chicken wings surrounding them, and watched the TV which was somehow still running, despite everything else in the apartment being powered off. The TV filled the room with a variety of sounds from moans to gunshots to fans in the crowd cheering. It was more chaotic than a food court vendor on a busy evening. But Mack still didn't like it.

Behind the couch was a dining room area which clearly wasn't used because a maze of silver server racks filled it. A bay window let cloudy light from the Valley into the apartment despite the crude efforts that had been made to cover it with packing material.

Two bedrooms were on opposite sides of the apartment. Each one was filled with pantry-sized server racks. The floor was covered in vinyl tubing that carried an emerald liquid in it, countless wires of every color of the rainbow, and a few stacks carry out boxes that, based on the logo, once had chicken wings in them.

If there was a recycler in this apartment it either didn't work, or the twins refused to use it.

Mack had a difficult time walking between the racks without stepping on wires. The only clear path was from the couch to the left-wing bathroom. Which was messy in its own right, but not with tubing and wires.

How the twins afforded an exterior mid-tower apartment was beyond Mack's comprehension, although neighbors likely said the same about Sophia and Mack affording such a high-tower penthouse.

Mack understood the idea of doing anything and everything to claw your way out of the bottom of the Valley. But rarely saw it paired with such laziness or disorganization. Even the messiest food court vendor had his own organization method.

If these fools had a method to their madness Mack couldn't spot it.

The TV screen covered the apartment's front wall and reached from the floor to the ceiling. It was segmented into a three-by-three grid with each cell playing a different show. Indulging in a single TV show would be a luxury, but these two were spoiled enough to watch nine.

At least two of the shows were porn, one was cartoon and the rest were action movies or sonicball matches. And to Mack each show seemed to be running at double speed, far too fast for Mack to process even a single show.

"How's the TV running?" Mack asked.

"Runs fine," Quai said.

Aside from Quai's microfuser, which was installed on the right side instead of the normal lefthand side, he was unenhanced. His brother had the same lack of 'hances and the strange microfuser placement. Both twins had black hair and a bowl cut, an approved 'glom style.

Despite the lack of 'hances, they were built like they could lift a hovercar. Broad shoulders like Phlox, big biceps and forearms. Their torso was shaped like a tortilla chip, not a physique you get by eating so many chicken wings and sitting on the couch.

They wore loose-fitting shorts that tied at the waist and a T-shirt that seemed too tight around their chest. Mack suspected sparing with either of them would be a challenge.

Quai's microfuser was flashing fast like he was about to overclock but his speech was still a slow drawl. He didn't have a grin or laugh at the joke, which made Mack curious if it was a jest or a serious answer. Not many strangers were bold enough, or dumb enough to joke with someone as heavily armed and armored as Mack.

"How are you powering the television?" Mack said in slow frustration.

"Lady came by yesterday," Quai said. "Told us to use it when the power went out."

"She had weird eyes but great tits," Lewd added.

A few of the sports channels changed to more erotic images. Mack groaned in frustration and disgust. The perverse acts displayed didn't bother Mack, but the gluttonous inhibition of the twins did.

The minister was no longer the most frustrating person in this operation. Honestly, for the past hour, he'd been fairly patient as the crew took the long walk down the stairs to the various apartments of the Hive Mind members. Mack split off from Phlox, Napalm, Devin, and Nikandr who had many more flights to descend. Hopefully, the minister could deliver the operating system before Nikandr got to the basement to plug the towermind in.

Mack had zip-tied the minister's hands together over his robes so it looked like he had big white tulips around his hands. The flowers made Mack think of and miss Sophia who would probably be waking up around now wondering where her partner was.

Hopefully, Mack would be home soon, and be able to take off their sweaty helmet and cramped body armor. They wanted to just be done with this damn tower. Although, if they solved the towermind's puzzle they'd wind up spending far more time in Excella as its new owner. At least then they could evict these slobs and give the large home to a family that needed the space.

"Power cable's over here," the minister said pointing at it with both hands since they were tied together.

The wire jutted out from the wall just under the TV. The socket was far bigger than what the TV needed. Because of this, the twins had built a makeshift converter out of spare wires and tape. Next to the messy converter was a massive round plug that matched in size to the wire Wyky installed. That wire clearly weaved around the couch and into the computer racks.

The solution was clear, but these twins were too stupid, or lazy, to solve it.

As technologically unadvanced as Mack was they knew what to do. They unplugged the TV.

The twins immediately started shouting curses and slurs at them.

Mack pulled both guns out of their holsters and aimed at the boys sitting on the couch. The quick movement was jarring to Mack's tender ribs which they'd almost forgotten about thanks to the concoction of pain meds Dasco administered.

With two guns pointed towards the couch the twins were smart enough to take the cue and shut up.

"We've got a job to do," Mack said. "Help us or get out of our way."

Lewd put his hands up in the air to surrender but stood up from the couch cautiously. His microfuser flashed slowly, which made Mack comfortable that he wasn't going to try to pull a fast one on them.

The brother approached the plug and Mack gave him space still pointing their pistol at him and his brother. Lewd unplugged the computer, then plugged in the converter. The TV came to life with its unsettling variety of noises.

Then Lewd plugged the computer into a part of the converter that looked to Mack like a mess of tape. It fit and the computer powered on once again. The hum of its fans and pumps competed with the sound of the TV. And to Mack's ears seemed to win.

Lewd backed away slowly and took his seat back on the couch.

"Let us know if you need anything else, bro," Quai said as his microfuser started flashing quicker to take in the copious TV programs.

"Of if you want to show us what else you're packin'," Lewd added with a smirk.

Mack fought the urge to put a bullet under his stupid hairline, they'd done worse for less. Mack holstered their guns under their arms and turned to the minister.

"How are you installing this operating system?" Mack asked. "You need a terminal or something?" They really wished Dasco could be here to help, but he was needed with the antenna array.

"I just need my hands freed," the minister replied.

Mack unsheathed the knife from their body armor and grabbed the minister's hands to cut the zip tie off. The left cuff was still red with blood but Mack noticed the tip of his pinky had reappeared, albeit a little pink like a birthmark.

Mack placed their knife on the minister's wrist and looked down on him expecting an explanation. Phlox wasn't one to skimp on a violent job. Which meant the minister had done the impossible.

"Galleria Valley doesn't have the best 'hances in the Central System," Liesel said with a shrug. "Don't believe all their propaganda," he added with a smile.

Suddenly the thin plastic zip tie felt inadequate. Sewage. The shotgun on their back felt inadequate.

"Would your heart patch itself up if I stabbed it?" Mack asked. "Would your brain cells relink if I put a bullet in your head?"

"After a while yes," Liesel said in a firm and flat tone. "Although I'd prefer not to test it, and it will make the delivery of the operating system difficult. Especially considering your timeline."

"And you came to bring these 'hances to the Valley? Execs are already too powerful. The board members would be unstoppable with this technology."

"I cannot share it," Liesel said. "The Elders entrusted it to me as their minister and I am to serve their justice across the Central System in repayment."

"And what justice are you serving here? You're working with Veronica. Trying to arrest me. All based on faulty data the 'gloms sent out."

"Right now I am here to give Bellina her independence back," Liesel replied. "It is against the Central System's codes to modify someone against their will and against the codes to preprogram them in a way that inhibits their free will. Baumein has clearly violated those on at least one occasion, likely more based on the number of towers in this Valley."

Mack cut the zip tie off the minister's wrists with a quick jerk, no longer concerned about nicking him with the sharp blade. Regardless of if he was on their side or not Mack knew when there was an enemy too far 'hanced to stand up against.

"Your codes mean nothing here in the Valley. The 'gloms run this place without oversight." If the minister hadn't figured that out growing up here, Mack doubted he'd realize it returning as an adult.

Liesel nodded as he walked up to a server rack and opened the sheet metal door with a loud clank.

Inside the pantry-sized computer were shelves filled with red and green circuit boards and large silver finned heat sinks with fans, or in some rare cases tubes, mounted to them.

"May I borrow that knife?" Liesel asked rolling up his left-hand sleeve.

Mack handed him the knife blade first then took a step back just outside his reach. They rested their hand under their armpit and on their gun.

The minister slit his wrist perpendicular to his arm and blood flowed around his forearm like a bracelet. Cables thick as veins grew out of his arm and linked to the circuitry of the computer.

Soon the blood stopped flowing and the opening in his wrist patched itself up. The new skin was a little red and raw, but healed much better than any scab Mack had. Small mounds grew around the wires that flowed from his wrists and it looked as harmless as pimples.

Mack looked at him, horrified and astonished.

He handed the bloody blade back handle first thanking Mack politely.

"You're able to interface with that?" Mack asked. Dasco would have a dozen questions to ask, he was the right one to know the technical aspects of it. All Mack knew was that this technology was outside their comprehension.

"My ASLAN score qualified me to be a towermind," Liesel said. If he was interfacing with the computer his mind wasn't bothered. He spoke at a normal speed, unlike someone overclocking their microfuser to multitask.

"I studied towerminds as much as I could using public information then disappeared down to the restricted basements to learn from the old mind in Pinemark Tower. His information was limited but I learned what I could, if only to reduce my anxiety around becoming a towermind."

"But you got off world..."

"And into the Ministry. Never thought I'd use the information again. But now serendipitously I'm free of Veronica's monitoring and available to help reprogram Bellina, this time with more free will."

"I'm starting to think very little is coincidental when it comes to that towermind," Mack said. And wondered if Bellina was the one person in the

Valley who deserved the title of queen.

"And the codes do apply to the Valley," the minister continued. "Conglomerates may control the Valley but the Elders control the gates between the stars. And my reports can cut Mandlestadt and Baumein off from those gates."

"You'll never get off the planet," Mack said. "It was a miracle you did it once. Twice is just impossible."

"I don't have to," Liesel said. "Bellina happened to build an independent antenna array that is powerful enough to transmit off-world. You want to send the Central System your own reports this computer—"

In the chaos of the TV's noises and astonishment of Liesel's 'hances Mack almost disregarded the sound on the door. Almost.

***

Mack noticed the chatter at the door over the sounds on the massive television because it happened at a normal speed. Instead of the high-pitched sped-up voices of action stars and porn models, Mack heard someone curse and then get scolded by someone else.

Mack slung the shotgun into their hands and turned their back on the minister who was tethered to the computer for the foreseeable future writing a new operating system for Bellina.

He was hidden well enough in the former dining room's maze of computers. Crossfire wouldn't reach him, not that being shot was apparently a threat to him. It'd be more difficult to repair the computers than the off-world minister.

"Badges at the door," Quai said over the sound of the TV. Two channels changed from sonicball to an action thriller with explosions and hand-to-hand combat.

"And a sexy-looking manti," Lewd added.

A stream from the door's fisheye peephole replaced an exploding space battle. The square lobby of the apartment complex, dimly lit by emergency lighting, was on full display.

Two badges placed explosives around the door with Veronica towering behind them. Most of her flesh was covered in tight-fitting body armor, but the exec still wasn't willing to put a helmet over her carefully styled hair. Her arms and legs were no longer deep purple but polished brass with five-fingered limbs and shockingly lifelike feet.

Mack's ribs could attest to the fact that even if the arms were normal-looking they could still pack a punch.

"Why are they setting a charge?" Mack asked. In the rare case of a power outage doors failed open for safety. Whose safety was still a mystery to Mack.

And even if the power wasn't out badges should have the authority to open mid-tower doors. Only senior execs had the money for privacy.

"Pops has the code and the power's not out here," Quai said.

"Remember bro?" Lewd added. "We kept it on for you."

"The lights are out," Mack said gesturing to the ceiling.

"Yeah," Quai said with a shrug. "Overhead lights are like super harsh, man."

"Are you gonna fight?" Mack asked. The charges would be set any second and the door would blow in momentarily. Bullet holes would not be good for the computer Liesel was wired into.

"Whatever happens happens," Quai said.

"We'll reboot from clones," Lewd added.

Mack could finally put the pieces together. These slobs hadn't clawed their way up from the Valley they'd fallen down from the penthouses. Someone still had the cash to afford them reboots though. The pair could be kids of some senior execs, hopefully not someone as powerful as a board member.

Mack pulled their helmet on and selected slugs with the thumb dial of the shotgun. It'd easily handle the badge's body armor this close. They kneeled in front of the TV and out of the way of the door's blast radius.

The cell of the screen Mack blocked played the fish-eye view from the peephole. It was more help than they expected from the twins. They watched the badges step back, and blow the door open.

The badges drew their sidearms and walked into the apartment hunched low. The pair was focused on the twins who sat on the couch more interested in the badges on TV than the ones in their apartment.

With two quick shots, Mack neutralized the badges. Their bodies slumped to the ground over the dislocated door. Mack trained their gun on the doorway waiting for Veronica to waltz in, unlikely to be so oblivious.

"I've got the 'hanced security team headed after your friends," Veronica said from the lobby. "But I wanted to take care of you myself. I hope my little Sophia isn't so bummed that she cancels our next appointment."

The peephole feed had disappeared when the door blew in, it was replaced with a sonicball match. Mack listened for the metal footsteps of the exec. But none came.

The square lobby of this apartment floor was an awful place to have a fight. The flat walls with scenic skyline photos provided no protection. The eight doors and elevator that surrounded the room would make it a shooting gallery if the residents this high up were bold enough to be armed.

Mack had been on the wrong side of an ambush too many times to not see this for the trap it was. They didn't want to be in their position, but if the roles were reversed they wouldn't want Veronica's exposed position either.

It'd be better for Veronica to come in here, tear up some equipment, and neutralize everyone including the minister.

But Veronica was an arrogant executive. Used to corporate sabotage, waves of backup, and fighting tin men who were trained to overclock during a fight.

Mack was just some thug from the bottom of the Valley. No backup. No 'hances. Just a few old-fashioned weapons they'd spent hours practicing with.

Veronica thought she could catch Mack like a rat in that wide-open lobby. They doubted the exec had ever tried to catch the elusive little things. Hell, she was probably too rich to ever have seen one.

But Mack had caught countless rats, on an empty belly, hungry for anything that didn't cost credits. It took time and practice. And getting bit a few times, even after the rodents were in your hands.

Mack turned around the doorway, their shotgun buried into the pit of their shoulder, and fired unrelentingly at Veronica. Mack kept the wall at their back, uninterested in a resident, or a hidden badge, catching them from behind. The emergency lighting of the lobby was enough to aim by and their shots went straight for Veronica's center of mass.

Veronica's microfuser flashed quickly and she blocked the shots with her brass arms. The slugs left silver dents, revealing that the polished brass coloring was merely a superficial veneer, typical for a Baumein.

By the time the shotgun ran out slugs the plates of Veronica's 'hanced arms were twisted and bent.

Mack could've switched to scattershot or beanbags but both would merely be a nuisance to the exec. Same went for the low-caliber pistols under Mack's arms. They slung the riffle behind them and the strap dug into their neck.

Mack pulled out their big knife, still covered in the minister's dried blood, and a smaller throwing knife. They held their fists just under their chin to block whatever the executive threw at them.

Veronica pulled the pistol from her hip, it was a cheap standard issue boxy thing that was a boring black. She aimed at Mack from across the lobby. It wasn't a difficult shot to make, anyone who'd spent time at a range could do it.

Each of Veronica's shots went wide and wild. They pinged off the doors and shattered the glass of the lobby's photographs. The closest one merely glanced off the shoulder pad of Mack's body armor.

It was clear that Veronica had never spent any time at a range. With specially 'hanced arms and a microfuser executives rarely missed. Their arms were programmed to be steady and microfusers calculated a precise trajectory.

But the inputs those calculations depended on were fed by delicate sensors inside of expensive 'hanced arms. Sensors that would be ruined, or at least uncalibrated, by a few rough shots from a shotgun slug.

Veronica threw the pistol across the room with the same inaccuracy her bullets had. She closed the distance with long and quick paces.

Up close Veronica's brass body was shorter than the purple one and barely reached Mack's neck. As someone tall and wide Mack was used to being bigger than their opponents.

And they knew not to underestimate Veronica's stature.

Three quick jabs from Veronica's arms landed on Mack's gut and took the air out of them. The arm's servos wouldn't be damaged that easily. The blows still had strength behind them.

Mack lunged at Veronica, eager to take her to the ground and wrestle. But the woman was too fast and dodged to Mack's left.

Mack put their arm down to guard their side and caught two of Veronica's punches on the armor of their left bicep. It didn't feel good, but it was better than breaking more ribs since the body armor's edges had the least protection.

Mack pivoted on their left foot and faced down the exec. Her spring-like hair bobbed with the inertia of her movements.

The wall that was once behind Mack was now to the pair's left. Mack faked a lunge forcing Veronica to dodge right.

Expecting the move Mack jabbed the small throwing knife into Veronica's side where her armor was weakest. The woman's arm came down to block the blow a moment too late. Mack stabbed into her flesh but Veronica's arm knocked Mack's grip off the knife before they could twist it.

Veronica's eyes went wide with fury. She showed no pain, as a cocktail of painkillers was likely being administered by her 'hances. She came at Mack with a quick flurry of punches.

They took the beating on their armor and helmet. Each blow to their head was a deafening thud. Every blow to their blocking arms or gut reminded Mack that their right ribs were far from healed.

The woman's pattern was incessant but repetitive. After a few cycles, Mack recognized the pattern of the preprogrammed boxing routine. Veronica probably didn't even spar, just bought a nice enough data pack that could defeat other preprogrammed fighters.

Mack stepped out of the way of the woman's right hook and into a blind spot the throw created.

Veronica carried on with two more punches into thin air and Mack hit the woman's head on the unguarded side. They hooked her right foot out from under her in the next moment.

The woman lay on the ground dazed and out of breath. Mack didn't waste a moment and tackled her.

Veronica tried to lift Mack up. The hydraulics of her legs strained but they weren't strong enough to lift Mack's weight.

In a tangled mess of arms and legs, Veronica reached for Mack's head pulling their helmet off in the process. Mack got both of their hands on a dented arm and pinned it to the ground.

Veronica's other arm tried to grip Mack's throat likely to choke them out but it was too small to wrap around their thick neck.

Mack pulled the dented plate of Veronica's arm off and sliced through every wire they could reach. They used the blunt side of their knife to wedge out any electronic they could find.

Damaging two suits in one day was an unexpected boon for Mack. It'd take Veronica a month to recover, maybe more. But she'd recover. Execs always recovered.

Something pricked Mack in the neck, where Veronica was pawing at them still trying to choke them out. Mack grabbed that arm off of their neck to disable it the same as the last.

They ripped off the covering of the arm. A needle receded into the now exposed inner workings. Mack clawed at it with her massive knife.

After a second of cutting out pieces of Veronica's arms, Mack's hands felt like they weren't under their control. It was like someone else had programmed them, and they refused to go where Mack wanted-ed. They didn't have the strength to pull out electronics anymore.

Mack didn't have the strength to hold themselves up. They fell on Veronica's armored chest.

The executive forced a cackle of a laugh. Her chest heaved under Mack trying to breathe under their weight.

Mack tried to curse but her words were slurred beyond under-standing. Mack had been drugged or poisoned. Some security crew would be here to pick up Veronica soon, dump Mack in the sewage, and destroy the computers in the twin's apartment.

The room, once dimly lit by emergency lighting, went bright. It was clear it was the end for Mack, they'd be facing the empty whiteness of eternity soon.

At the edge of Mack's fading vision, they saw the minister rush out of the apartment.

Veronica was flailing against Mack trying to push them off with arms that wouldn't follow her commands.

The minister took the sharp knife out of Mack's hand. Mack unwillingly gave the weapon up, too weak to fight back.

The minister slit Mack's wrist with the knife.

Mack never should've trusted that man. Likely did as much good as seawater to Bellina and her computers.

But Bellina, Excella Tower, and the Syndicate as a whole would be someone else's problem. Maybe Phlox would wind up on top. Hopefully, Sophia would get out, or at least stay safe.

Mack knew their partner would make the most of it. That's what you had to do coming up from the bottom of the Valley.

***

Mack shielded their eyes from the harsh overhead light that shone down from the ceiling. They smelled the spice of chicken wings but didn't hear the unsettling variety of noises they expected to come with it.

Laying on the twin's stained couch Mack looked at the door, still blown off its hinges. They reached for their gun and wrapped their hand around the grip.

A metal hand rested on their arm before they could draw it.

"It's okay. We're safe," someone said.

Mack looked up to see Phlox standing over them and the minister perched on the arm of the couch. The twins were leaning against a wall staring off into space, focused on whatever was playing on their microfusers.

Mack sat up, uneager to be prone in the middle of a merger. Their feet knocked over a stack of empty takeout boxes and their head swam.

"You'll be good as new in another half hour," Liesel said. He was pecking away at the keyboard of a hand terminal. "Once the power came on Phlox came up here. Otherwise, you'd still be lying in the hallway."

"If the power's on backup security'll be here soon," Mack said. They pulled their gun out and rested it on their lap ready to fire at whoever came to the door. Their wrist was sore. They looked at it and a small red line ran perpendicular to their forearm.

"Bellina has reconfigured the ALMS system to keep anyone hostile to the Syndicate at bay," Phlox said.

The ALMS system was once used to overclock anyone who entered Excella Tower and wasn't associated with Baumein. The change didn't seem like a difficult modification. But if Bellina could do that she was truly free of Baumein's control.

And it likely led to a lot of brain-dead execs. Not that Mack saw that as a great loss.

"Baumein employees and residents weren't affected were they?" Mack asked. Bellina would be no better than a board member with that level of tyranny.

"As long as they're not hostile to the new acquisition they're safe," Phlox said. "It's a good thing the minister had the antidote to Veronica's poison. Now you get to run an entire tower."

"What happened to proper channels and all that?" Mack asked Minister Liesel. "And not modifying people against their will?"

Mack was glad to be alive but didn't appreciate having whatever 'hances the minister was using in their body. Who knew what control he gained over Mack by installing it.

"If I recall correctly 'proper channels ain't done nothing for me lately,'" The minister said with a grin "It'll be out of your system in a few hours. You didn't get the full effects, so try to keep all your fingers attached."

"I'm sending off a message to the Elders now to embargo both Baumein and Mandlestadt from using the gates," Liesel said.

"Don't." Mack shifted the gun in their lap towards him.

If Liesel noticed he didn't react but he did look at Mack curious to hear them out.

"All it will do is hurt the people at the bottom of the Valley. You cut off the 'glom's ability to operate they'll just extract more from the people in the Valley to make sure they stay comfortable. They're not interested in improving."

"This Valley is a pit of human rights violations," Liesel replied. "The Elders could send a hundred ministers to clean it up."

"Until the 'gloms go find some other planet to sap resources out of. How long will it take for someone to find their way out of that pit and into the Ministry?"

"What do you propose?" Liesel sounded unsatisfied but resigned.

"New leadership," Mack said.

"We can't interfere with conglomerate operations at that level," Liesel said.

Mack suspected that if the sacred Elders really wanted to they could do a whole lot more than they did. But that was off-world politics. All Mack cared about was the Valley, and the exploited people in it.

"We have a tower," Mack said.

"For now," Phlox scoffed.

She was right. Excella may have held for centuries as a Baumein stronghold. Even with inside help Mandlestadt couldn't take it today.

But Mack would have both 'gloms against them.

Since the dust settled after the War of Acquisition every tower in the Valley was owned by either Baumein or Mandlestadt. Mack knew the 'gloms would fight to keep that dichotomy.

And another war would be bad for every citizen in the Valley.

"The Syndicate wants recognition as a conglomerate," Mack said. "And protection from whatever the 'gloms are about to throw at us."

Liesel laughed, surprised by Mack's statement. Mack was surprised too. One of the last things they ever wanted to be was the head of a conglomerate. The destruction and chaos those leaders caused was unforgivable. Next, they'd be getting a microfuser installed and become a tin man.

Could Mack be able to be any different than the execs? The Syndicate helped people as best it could, but there were limitations. A distributed network of criminals could only do so much.

"Can you do it?" Mack asked. "You're so eager to embargo them, tell them if they go after Excella then you'll embargo. It won't remove them from our backs but it'll force them to be covert about it."

"The Elders can't back a known criminal organization," Liesel said.

"You saw the Clarvo data. Plus, I can introduce you to a hundred families grateful for food we smuggled in and the lifesaving drugs we provided. Deep docs who've installed prosthetics to people the 'gloms fired for underperformance."

"And the people whose fingers you've severed," Liesel asked with a smile.

"If they know what's good for them they'll keep their mouth shut," Phlox said, unhelpfully.

"You can talk with them if you want they see eye to eye with us now," Mack said. At least the ones that were still around.

"Regardless," Mack continued, "your data's bad minister. Protect us, for a quarter or two and we'll send out better data. Then you'll see who the criminals are."

Liesel shook his head. Stood up from the couch arm and paced around the messy apartment. Mack holstered their gun as they waited.

"I can give the Syndicate probationary recognition," Liesel said. "But you'll have to apply for permanent recognition. It's not easy. And you'll have to do things through the proper channels now."

The minister reached out to shake Mack's hand. No contracts, no paperwork, just an old-fashioned agreement.

No one followed proper channels in the Valley. You'd be ruined by the competition if you did. But maybe it was time for that to change.

They shook the minister's hand. "I can do that."

It wouldn't be easy, but Mack would make the most of it.

They always had.

Also By Nicholas Licalsi

Path of the Bearers and Other Stories

An AI with the potential to predict the future must uncover its creator's inexplicable disappearance. A scientist must reveal the limitations of his high profile project to while his investor takes them on a joyride through an asteroid field. A writer travels to a pocket dimension to find time to write, but something sinister follows.

Visit seedy space station bars, distant planets where dormant aliens rest. One wrong decision could ruin humanity's chances of surviving among the stars.

This book is your portal to explore the cosmos and beyond...
https://books2read.com/PathOfTheBearersAndOtherStories

Bleeding Rock

Mauve, a talented mechanic, always dreamed of leaving her satellite home. So she didn't think twice before signing up for a routine planetary survey.

Mauve awakes from the landing hanging upside down. Clearly something went wrong. She will need all her mechanical knowledge to get the mission back on track.

But the crash landing is only the start of her troubles.

With her AI assistant Mauve must use everything she discovers on this alien world to escape it.

<u>If you enjoy science fiction exploration stories with elements of horror then you'll love Bleeding Rock!</u>

https://books2read.com/BleedingRock

A Trial of Rock and Rope

Upon his death, Ferrun Monteiro wakes up in the afterlife. Instead of building paradise the gods have designed a challenge.

To escape the afterlife Ferrun must reach the top of a mountain with a boulder tied to his ankle.

Yet not a single soul has completed this seemingly simple trial.

Unperturbed, Ferrun faces the god's challenge head on. Follow him on his odyssey through the afterlife.

If you enjoy dreaming about the afterlife, you'll enjoy A Trial of Rock and Rope.

https://books2read.com/ATrialOfRockAndRope

About the Author

Nicholas Licalsi was born and raised outside of Fort Worth, in the beautiful but backwards state of Texas. Growing up, he was fascinated with science fiction and fantasy. This interest led to pursuing a degree in engineering and participating in multiple robotics competitions. After a successful enough career in software development Nicholas spends his time trying to trick his overactive imagination into paying the bills while he satiates his dog's need to be pet.

You can connect with me at: https://stepintotheroad.com

Get updates about my upcoming books at: https://stepintotheroad.com/signup

www.ingramcontent.com/pod-product-compliance
Lightning Source LLC
Chambersburg PA
CBHW031950240626
47153CB00003B/926